The Legend of the Haunted Bus Route.

Aarthi Gailine

TABLE OF CONTENTS......

THE LEGEND OF THE HAUNTED BUS ROUTE..2

MY NEIGHBOR IS A MONSTER...7

BEYOND THE INDIANGRASS, WHAT LURKS...23

MY BOYFRIEND. 59

JUST ONE MORE TIME 62

HEATHENBERRY FOREST'S WISHING WELL..80

EVEN THOUGH I LIVE ALONE, THERE IS A WOMAN ON MY COUCH. 93

SOMETHING IS KEEPING AN EYE ON ME, AND IT ISN'T AN ANGEL. 100

THE IRISH COUNTRYSIDE IS BEING HAUNTED BY AN ANCIENT HORROR. 123

The Legend of the Haunted Bus Route

Operating a coach. I'm unsure exactly how people that are numerous they could do that once they had been kids, but the one thing I am aware for sure is the fact that I did. I began exactly what is discovering could, and soon, We became a bus motorist. In the beginning everything felt very nice. Nice buses being modern-day friendly coworkers and passengers, and lovely roads, well, aside from one.

It had been a path this is certainly residential district linked the biggest market of the town We worked directly into a little town on the outskirts. Few people like going folks utilized that path, and buses would frequently operate empty along with it. I always liked getting together with the passengers, so I didn't would you like to drive on a route which barely had any, at least that is what I'd tell everybody, but truth be told, there is certainly another explanation. Every motorist that has been assigned towards the change on that route moved madly within times of working on it a night. I never ever understood why that kept happening, and I hoped I would personally never ever learn, regrettably, I did. The motorist who had been expected to take the move declined to come to work evening. The route would have to be operated, us to it instead so they assigned. An integral part of me personally wished to prevent coming to exert effort and make a justification up for perhaps not showing up, but another element of me ended up being like:

"I'm being ridiculous; you'll find nothing incorrect aided by the route, every little thing will likely be alright. "

The shift ended up being taken by myself. It had been cold temperatures so that it had been getting dark rather early. I came to the terminus when you look at the populous city center and took over from my coworker. I made two loops in the route and transported, maybe, 10 passengers as a whole, and also they were just taking a trip a few stops and would log off prior to the suburbs will be reached by the coach. I became making my loop that is third on path and my coach had been empty. I could only scarcely see in the front of my coach compliment of my headlights, but away from them there was clearly absolutely nothing but barely noticeable silhouettes of leafless trees and old abandoned houses around me had been total darkness. Winter ended up being only starting, and there isn't any snow however, it to glow at night and then make the trip slightly less creepy thus I performed have even. It very nearly appeared like I was in an endless void that is black. At one point I viewed my mirror and saw a female in a dress this is certainly long a man sitting in the back of the bus.

"I don't keep in mind all of them getting on.", I was thinking.

I was able to convince myself around me personally and contemplate the reason why my coworkers would get mad after operating on this path, that I merely performed notice them getting on that I must have already been preoccupied by seeing the creepy darkness. I had reached the stop this is certainly last. I had a couple of minutes before my next departure, I would typically put it to use for a bathroom break, but it had been therefore dark outside that We dreaded i may get lost I quickly noticed the lady and also the man during the straight back, I thought possibly they got on the wrong coach and performed realize that this is the final stop if we left my coach, but. I moved over to the relative back once again to tell them, but when I got near, the lady looked up at me. She together with man turned white, as well as the woman allow a horrifying screech out. Simply then loads of other individuals showed up around me, all dressed in classic clothes, and all sorts of as pale as the girl and also the man. Each of them began screaming, I covered my ears. Simply compared to the guy who was simply sitting beside the woman up to this real point got up and walked up to me . He grabbed their cool hand to my mind and pulled it nearer to his. A look had been got by myself into his eyes, and I'll remember the thing I saw, it absolutely was therefore distressful that I'm not really sure simple tips to explain it. The guy whispered into my ear in a voice that is raspy

"You're perhaps not the one! "

After that everyone disappeared. I examined my watch and saw that it was deviation time. I experienced no longer people for the others of my move, paranormal or regular. We continued working on that route for the week that is next I lasted more than the motorists just who labored on it before me personally. Each night the matter that is same happen. You'll genuinely believe that after a little while I'd get used to it, and it would no longer be therefore scary, but that has been maybe not the entire instance, it scared me every time. Fortunately I haven't been assigned to that particular path ever since then. I managed to remain sane, I additionally been able to find out just who the social people I was encountering had been.

Evidently, a tragic accident happened in that town several years ago, a bus crashed and a fire which burned down all the village started, all of the individuals on board that bus lived truth be told there, although not a single one of them survived the accident, today their particular spirits haunt that little bit of the coach route, to locate the driver who was driving the bus in the nights the accident for they just go away so they could get payback, but when they note that a motorist is not the driver they're looking. Despite the fact that they do no damage, this is certainly real one look to their eyes is enough to make a driver ask becoming assigned to some other course, enough appears plus the motorist goes mad. We still have nightmares to this day. I wake up covered in perspiration. I don't know then and there if I ever get assigned to that horrible route once again if I'll ever conquer those activities, but anything I do know is that I'm quitting my job appropriate.

My neighbor is a monster.

I'm writing this diary to collect my ideas and leave a record for my children, so they can understand just why I've taken these actions. Because, whenever all's said and finished, every thing i actually do will be protect my loved ones and also to make certain they will have a home to once get back to that is all done. We don't know if I'll survive the battles forward, but i am aware my legacy shall live on.

It all began per week ago – a mere 7 days for my life that is whole to apart. That's as he moved into the Johnson that is old spot less than 2 hundred yards from my house. I don't understand what the entity is exactly – a demon, cryptid, or something else…Who can state? All i am aware is it's a monster – a beast with harmful intention.
Their reign of terror started very little a lot more than low level intimidation, but shortly escalated into one thing a lot more dangerous and sinister. We arrived residence one evening week that is final spotted the dim light shining through the old farm's window. I thought this is strange.

Mr Johnson had been the owner of the farm for well over thirty years, but he died of a heart attack last winter. The farmhouse this is certainly old been vacant since his death, as his distant family members continue to argue over the property. The light we saw that caused me some issue because I was thinking somebody had broken in – a squatter or partying teenagers perhaps night.

I vowed to check on it out the next day, but I confess as I ended up being concerned about boring everyday things such as for example work, my marriage, and looking following the kids so it slipped my mind. It might probably have finished here however it performed.

The next evening was when things started to take a turn this is certainly sinister. The screams began around midnight – a squealing that is high-pitched from the old Johnson spot. The din was horrifying; anything comparable to a banshee's wail. It continued for hours, the sound that is awful through my skull, almost operating me personally insane.

The matter that is strangest is the fact that no-one else could hear it – maybe not my partner, my boy, or my daughter…not even dog! From the screaming within my partner to be heard within the god-awful din and she just looked I happened to be crazy at me like. I couldn't understand it at the time. Had been the monster choosing to torment me, and only me? I couldn't believe this was the truth.

Perhaps We have a feeling that is 6th an instinct which alerts myself when my family has nin danger, even when the hazard is supernatural in beginning. On that first-night we armed myself with a baseball bat and headed out, indicating to face whatever was creating this noise that is horrific. But i did son't ensure it is.

I obtained within 50 yards for the farmhouse before collapsing to my legs, experiencing like my mind was going to explode. Fighting through my discomfort, we looked up during the home, seeing a shadow that is dark at an upper window, glaring down at me personally with menacing intent. I possibly couldn't make any functions away, but I understood during my heart that the being viewing me had been pure evil.

I swore the creature could be heard by myself laughing cruelly as I crawled returning to my house, the pain sensation during my skull slowly subsiding.

It played out of the same throughout the next nights that are few. I did son't understand how to stop the sound this is certainly hideous so I took to putting on noise-reducing headsets. We reckoned the monster would stay static in Johnsonn't'sJohnson n't's farmhouse forever. Undoubtedly he was only utilising the derelict building as a staging post, softening me personally up with psychological warfare before starting his attack upon my family.

The daylight was invested by myself hours organizing – barricading windows and doorways and building a collection of do-it-yourself weapons. I believe in relying on my personal mettle in place of calling law enforcement in terms of house defence.

My spouse ended up beingn't happy though. We had a row that is blazing the 3rd day, and she took the children together with dog inside her automobile, saying she was going to stick to her mama until 'I came ultimately back to my senses'. I happened to be annoyed she didn't believe me along with her and couldn't understand why. All things considered, I was doing all this work to safeguard her and the children. But we rationalized because they is out of harm's way when the shit hit the lover it was to find the best. No intention had been had by me personally in operating away nonetheless.

Last night, the screaming ended quite instantly at about 3am. I'd gotten so used into the din this is certainly terrible within my ears and thus need to have thought relieved, but We knew it was likely the relax before the storm – a prelude to some thing far worse.

We ended up most of the lights within my house and took address behind my front that is barricaded door holding my loaded shotgun tightly when I peeked out through the letterbox. We believed a foreboding feeling of dread as I observed the lonely country lane right away from my residence, a narrow road shrouded in darkness, aided by the only illumination coming from the performers above therefore the dim light coming from Johnson's old farmhouse.

I must have perched indeed there for around three to four hours, shivering from the cool and something worse – a horror this is certainly primal. I tried my best to remain alert, but I happened to be exhausted, and so my eyes begun to droop. Then again it absolutely was heard by me– the noise of hefty footsteps, slowly but surely making their particular way down the lane.

I happened to be awake this is certainly large an instant, leaping to interest when I grabbed your hands on my firearm, opening the doorway ever so slightly and poking the barrel out through the gap. The tension was intolerable together with terror I thought ended up being practically overwhelming when I waited when it comes to monster to emerge. My hand was poised regarding the trigger. My arms shook, but I became determined to make the bastard away, in the event that chance arose.

Eventually, the animal showed up at the top of the laneway, nevertheless hidden into the shadows and about 50 yards approximately from my entry way. I could see little when you look at the dark – simply a shape which appeared to be a man, it absolutely was anything but although I knew. We silently begged because i needed to look at monster's true kind, but therefore I could get a clear shot in the bastard for him to come closer, maybe not.

But he did actually have anticipated my program, throughout the void as he stopped lifeless in the middle of the trail, glaring at myself. We understood the creature could see me personally and I could feel his look that is hateful upon. Then he started to laugh – a cackle that is terrifying filled the night atmosphere.

The sound had been horrific, even worse than the screams associated with nights being previous. This becoming this is certainly evil mocking me – laughing inside my discomfort. Instantly, my anxiety turned to anger when I pulled the trigger, firing buckshot throughout the void. But my target had been standing just out of range, and he barely even reacted into the shot, instead continuing to laugh in open mockery, until he eventually fired up their heels and calmly stepped back-up the lane, returning to the abandoned farmhouse he'd changed into his hellish nest.

I became left terribly shaken because of the encounter and remained inside my post until, expecting a follow up attack dawn. Nevertheless the beast ended up being done for the, and I existed to start to see the morning night.

So, this brings me as much as time. This might be my story. My fight. Using this point forwards I will report my battles that are daily this beast. I'll prepare during the and battle after dark, and We won't end until one of us is lifeless day.

Monday

I invested the daylight hours creating traps along the laneway and across the fields which can be adjacent. Each day I constructed up a punji pitfall affixed to a tree trunk and set a visit cable across the laneway that is slim. My mid-day had been occupied by building a homemade pipeline bomb, that we intend to utilize as an hand this is certainly improvised, if the beast gets close enough.

My anxiety returned as darkness dropped, but we felt more confident because of the preparations I'd made throughout the day. For enough time that is very first this nightmare began, we dared to consider I'd attained top of the hand, however I did something stupid which put me personally in grave danger. I fell asleep.

It must has been anticipated by myself truly. I'dn'tI'dn't rested for days most likely, and adrenaline that is pure only just take you to date. I happened to be perched up against the barricades watch that is maintaining my energy eventually provided method, and I closed my eyes. We don't discover how long I was asleep, but I was caught because of the beast off guard.

I awoke to screaming, the banshee-like wailing associated with previous evenings, except louder, since the sound that is terrible emanating from right outside of my door. I jumped-up in terror, instinctively grabbing for my shotgun in a attempt that is hopeless protect myself. But it had been currently too late.

My barrier was crushed through by the beast like it was made of report. An additional later, he used power that is immense smash within my solid pine home, knocking me straight down in the act. I happened to be virtually crushed because of the weight associated with the home falling to my nerves, experiencing a-sharp pain at the back of my mind when I hit the surface that is tough. I destroyed consciousness a second later, nevertheless the final experience I had before every little thing went black colored had been the noise regarding the creature's laughter that is sadistic.

The first rays of sunlight were noticeable because of the right time i regained consciousness. My mind was nevertheless throbbing when I struggled to pull my bruised body out from underneath the fallen door. Honestly, I happened to be amazed to possess survived the attack. The beast had gotten the better of me and I'd already been completely at their mercy, and however he hadn't hit the blow that's fatal. I am able to just deduce he desires to prolong my suffering. But my nemesis has made a mistake that is deadly in which he needs killed myself whenever he had the chance.

So, we pulled myself together, bandaged my head, downed some painkillers, and returned to focus.

Tuesday

After repairing the door that is forward I put much more traps during the day, searching a gap and lining the underside with sharpened surges, before covering it with branches and leaves. Next, I prepared a supply of Molotov cocktails, making use of alcohol this is certainly old and petrol siphoned from my fuel container.

My head was still throbbing, and I also performedn't like to exposure passing out again, so I got a hours which can be few to charge before the night's struggle. We stood shield in the door, anticipating a repeat associated with night's this is certainly earlier, but my nemesis changed his strategies, toying beside me and testing my defenses.

He circled the house, pushing me from screen to screen. All I could see was a black shadow beyond the treeline, which prompted us to use my weapon to attempt pot shots. But we never hit him, in which he laughed in open mockery every right time i missed. I realised far too late what their plan had been. I became desired by him to expend my method of getting ammunition. And then he nearly succeeded, leaving me with just two shells.

Pangs of panic struck me as of this true point as I considered my next move. In the event that monster broke in again – that he was truly effective at doing – I wasn't sure the bastard could possibly be taken by me. We considered making a stand that is final as well as burning up the house straight down around me...a desperate 'scorched earth' tactic to reject my nemesis their last success. But this didn't show needed, due to the fact creature broke off his attack, making me to fight another day.

Without doubt he would like to prolong my misery for at least another night. But I've got a surprise waiting for you for the bastard, because I'm perhaps not planning to play by his guidelines any more.

Wednesday (mid-day)

I would like to report my thoughts and feelings before darkness drops, as I have an atmosphere that is bad today could be my last on this globe. We phoned my spouse today. It performedn't get well. I recently wished to talk to the small children, but she declined to put them regarding the phone, saying I would only disturb all of them. I lost my mood and shouted she hung-up on myself at her, and. I attempted calling straight back, nonetheless it moved right to the answering machine.

I just don't understand the lady anymore. Doesn't she realize I'm doing all of this on her behalf and our children? Then who will if i don't protect our home? I happened to be upset following the debate but knew I'd to place it behind me while focusing from the task at hand. Every little thing shall make contact with normal once this beast is defeated.

Nonetheless, we cannot escape the terrible thought that I could die as a result of my nemesis that I may maybe not win this battle. But at least in the event that worst happens I'll have actually stood my ground, and my children may take pleasure in once you understand we fought for all of them.

Some way this will be over before dawn. I'm tired of hiding away and waiting for this bastard to come quickly to me personally. Tonight, I'm going from the offensive.

Wednesday (night)

I'm hurt...bad. Somehow we managed to get straight back in the home, but I don't understand how I've that is long got I pass out due to loss of blood. I considered phoning for help...perhaps the ambulance shall get here in time. But you, I'm ashamed. The 'monster' is lifeless, that's a certainty. But my triumph is a hollow one. I don't know how this took place, but i have to attempt to explain, for the sake of my kids.

I launched my assault right after dusk, advancing along the laneway and over the industries, armed with my shotgun and carrying the pipeline bomb I'd constructed over the previous times which can be few. The awful sound started nearly just myself, reverberating inside of my head as I stepped out of my entry way, the banshee-like screaming which deafened.

It absolutely was nearly unbearable, but I was determined to fight through the pain sensation. I happened to be virtually crawling through the dirt for the last 50 yards, my head pounding like my head ended up being about to explode. I virtually passed out because of the pain, but somehow I kept going, my hurting eyes concentrated upon my objective – the dilapidated home this is certainly old into a hell residence.

We saw him into the window, a shadow that is dark me, emitting the hellish sound in an attempt to break myself. I experienced a surge of righteous anger with all my might as I approached the home... raising my bomb, lighting the fuse, and tossing it. The pipeline bomb travelled through the fresh air, smashing the glass and landing inside of the house. An additional later on and the unit detonated with a great time this is certainly deafening.

The figure this is certainly shadowy retreated from the window and emitted a howl of the things I took to be discomfort. I cried call at victory, realizing that I'd finally gotten the higher of the bastard. Rushing forwards, we banged in the home that is front of house and stormed around with my shotgun in hand. We quickly discovered a trail of flesh bloodstream, following it further in to the homely residence, scarcely acknowledging my environments as I concentrated entirely upon my quarry.

Spotting motion in the place of my attention, we looked to see a figure fleeing down a corridor this is certainly darkened. Performing on instinct, we increased my shotgun, aimed and fired, experiencing the kick-back that is heavy my neck. We saw my nemesis fall following the buckshot tore through his back.

I can't describe the ecstasy I believed for the reason that brief moment, having eventually bested my adversary. I practically skipped along the corridor and so I could examine their body. Reaching out with both-hands, I switched his heavy, lifeless body over, looking to start to see the face of an inhuman monster...But, to my shock and horror, we saw a man.

A normal individual, no different he had been not any longer breathing from myself, except their eyes had been shut and. It struck me so difficult for the reason that awful minute, i'd killed just what looked like an innocent when I realised. But exactly how could this be possible? This man couldn't are the one harassing me over the past evenings being few. It was impossible!

I unexpectedly believed rather ill, retreating through the corpse as I scanned the encompassing corridor in detail for the time this is certainly first. The thing I saw wasn't the abandoned, decrepit old farmhouse we anticipated to find but rather a lived-in house – a family group dwelling that is comfortable. We looked to a table with a lamp, getting a neatly framed picture. The picture inside had been that of a man along with his family members; their partner as well as 2 kiddies that are younger. Therefore the man I'd shot was the paternalfather when you look at the picture.

I'd killed a grouped family man; somebody exactly like me. My mind was rotating and I also believed as I dropped the image and retreated back down the corridor, out of the human anatomy of this man I'd savagely killed like I would personally vomit. I couldn't keep to stay in that homely household any more, not after just what I'd done.

I began to operate, rushing away through the door I'd kicked in before sprinting across the industries which are darkened. I could hear screaming want it ended up being before behind me, although not. It absolutely was a lady and children sobbing out in grief. They'd discovered his human body.

Tears had been rolling down my cheeks when I fled from the scene like a coward. I suppose I became however in a situation of surprise, We unknowingly dropped into my very own trap, piercing my leg on a sharpened surge because I forgot in regards to the pit right in front of my door, and. Somehow I prevented impaling myself, but I sliced my thigh began and open bleeding like a pig. I've was able to pull myself out and use a tourniquet that is makeshift temporarily halting the flow of bloodstream. We don't determine if I'll shed consciousness or whether the injury shall come to be infected. Or maybe I'll only end it all, making use of my shotgun that is final layer blow my head off. I don't think I am able to carry on after this, not after killing a man who is certainly innocent.

I'm trying to know how this occurred. Was I fooled by some type or kind of black-colored magic? Or had been it all within my mind? It scarcely matters today, I guess. I was thinking I was doing the point that is right battling to protect my residence and my family, but maybe I happened to be the beast all along. God forgive me because we doubt someone else will.

It was very nearly Halloween. Leafless tree branches swayed into the sharp breeze. The grey sky is overcast on yet another day of rain. Yellow-grey cornstalks flitted past, and lifeless leaves spread once the huge, brown Buick transported us along the nation road this is certainly bare.

I seemed ahead to witnessing Granny, even I was sticking with her if she'd be working more often than not. Grandpa consented to view myself through the day. He obtained a stipend from a relative back damage he received in the military. It wasn't much, but between the check that is monthly Granny working it absolutely was enough. He always liked the company. I would personally be told by him tales about his time in the army and he understood the funniest jokes We heard. He allow me to explore the bare industries and little forests near their residence as he performed his everyday tasks like washing the house. I looked ahead to looking for arrowheads, playing on hay bales, climbing trees... Maybe not that last one.

The disadvantage that is just my visit ended up being I had to blow it with my cousin, Kasey. My grandparents became her guardians that are legal her mom left. Dad and mother never ever explained where she moved. I worried she could have gone to prison or ended up like those personal individuals on Unsolved Mysteries. I would have experienced sorry for Kasey me anytime the grownups weren't around if she didn't bully.

"We're only likely to be gone three days because of this company refuge, one to behave your self. so I expect" Dad looked at me within the rearview mirror. "I don't would like you within the hospital again."

"Don't worry, I'll be good."

Mom switched in her seat to face myself. You right back something special for great behavior"If you're a great guy, maybe we'll bring. You'll make sure he's good, won't you Teddy?" She held my bear this is certainly stuffed and him nod their head like a puppet. I happened to be old enough to learn Teddy wasn't carrying it out himself, but We played along.

"Teddy gets a present-day also, appropriate? Once and for all bear-haviour?"

Mother beamed before turning around. "Of course, sweetie."

The once smooth, peaceful ride unexpectedly became harsh and loud as dad's car transitioned from pavement to the soil and gravel leading the rest of the method to my grandparents' house. Granny would take me on lengthy walks down this stretch of roadway, and I also would look for little rocks that are round called "Indian Beads". I showed some to my first-grade instructor, Mrs. Smith and she said these people were really fossils from a plant that is primitive.

I noticed the abandoned home on the place once we found a stop at a four-way intersection. It absolutely was the sole household this is certainly neighboring my grandparents for miles. All of the 12 months it absolutely was totally concealed from view because of the trees and vines that are overgrown the chain website link fence. Nonetheless, after most of the leaves had fallen, i really couldn't distinguish much other than the chipping paint and porch that is wrap-around. A few house windows on the ground this is certainly top within the trees, their particular displays torn and shutters unsecured.

"Somebody actually ought to fix that location up." Mom said.

"Too belated for the," Dad said. "The roofing is caved in. It's maybe not safe."

"That's a shame. It must be over a hundred yrs old."

A clear area arrived into view after the fence line towards the abandoned home. It probably belonged to whoever had the house, nevertheless the thing that is only expanded with it were groups of Indiangrass, cattails, & most notably, a huge oak-tree in the exact middle of the area. It absolutely was so huge two grown-ups could reach all the n't way around it. A number of the limbs were reduced enough they could be achieved by me without having any assistance. I nearly forgot all the enjoyable we had playing in this industry once I understood my grandparents' house had been getting into view.

Grandpa had been smoking a tobacco from the porch that is front we pulled up. He was jolted from some reverie as Maggie, the laboratory that is black up and barked, wagging her end. The automobile wasn't also parked before I bolted out the door.

"Grandpa!" I went to hug him. We almost knocked him over. He laughed on the porch railing while he steadied himself. A tube of grey cinders dropped from the tip of his tobacco cigarette as he laughed.

"What will they be feeding you, Bucko? You will get bigger every right time we see you."

I shrugged, in which he discrete another laugh that is loud. "You understand what? Some cartoons were got by myself recorded for you!"

"Really?" We only got stations which can be local my house. The actual only real cartoons were the ones on PBS, and that was only if they weren't broadcasting home this is certainly boring shows.

He beamed. "Your grandma left the videotapes next to the television for you personally."

Mom and Dad came up to your porch, Dad because of the suitcase, Mom with Teddy. Grandpa bent right down to whisper one thing for me. Under your pillow." We hid something for you"

"Really? What-is-it?"

Me personally Teddy"Don't you spoil the man, dad," Mom handed.

"Spoil him? It's Halloween is not it Johnny?"

"Uh-Huh!"

"well, we hate to down drop him and run, but we do want to get going." Dad looked over his watch. "Johnny, you act today."

"i am going to."

We hugged my parents goodbye. They waved because they backed out from the driveway and pulled on the road. The big vehicle that is brown vanished in a cloud of dirt. We picked up my luggage and went inside.

"I'll maintain there in a minutes that are few" Grandpa said, deciding in to the grass seat and sipping his coffee. "I just want to complete this newsprint article."

I wandered through the family area and saw the VHS tapes only like grandpa said. One of many labels read "Speed Racer". I possibly couldn't wait to look at them. I set my suitcase on the ground next to the bunk bed when I got to the visitor bed room. Kasey always slept when you look at the top bunk which left me personally on the base. We set Teddy down and reached beneath the pillow. To my shock there is absolutely nothing. Puzzled, the pillow had been moved by myself and discovered the location underneath had been bare. I seemed underneath the sleep thinking possibly whatever Grandpa left for me personally had fallen on to the floor.

"Looking with this?" Kasey was dangling ugly through the bunk this is certainly top. She dangled a bag of assorted candy while biting down a piece of taffy.

"Hey! Grandpa said that was said to be for me!"

"Not anymore." She chomped the mess that is sticky her lips between words. A tootsie that is few fell from the case as she rummaged for something different.

"Oh, you can have those." She grimaced. "I don't like those anyhow."

I found the pieces of candy from the flooring and put all of them in the base bunk.

"They're much better than absolutely nothing,as we put Teddy in addition to the pillow" I thought.

"Why couldn't you merely opt for your parents?" Kasey ended up being scowling, nonetheless upside down.

"They're happening a company trip," I said. "Kids aren't allowed."

"Whatever," Kasey said, vanishing on the side of the sleep. We wondered if Kasey was going to be this real way the entirety of my stay. No, she couldn't be. Perhaps not with all the grown-ups around. Even if they weren't she could often be alright. Maggie's barking from the porch interrupted the idea. Through the window next to the bunkbed, we saw Granny's automobile pulling up the driveway and in to the lean-to carport behind the house. We ran through the kitchen and out the general back door to satisfy her. Kasey shoved myself apart into the carport as she rushed past myself.

"Granny, Granny! You'll never guess what i did so in school today!"

"I'm sure it had been wonderful lover." Granny fumbled an cigarette that is unlit her lips.

"Hi, Granny!"

"Well, hi, Johnny!" Granny hugged me personally. "Are you hungry for some cheeseburgers?"

"You result in the best cheeseburgers in the world, Granny." She smiled as I stated this and slammed the door that is right back behind us. It absolutely was an old door, possibly area of the house's construction that is initial. The latch did work most of n't the time, and there clearly was about an inch between your bottom regarding the door together with limit. I remembered how frightened We had been summer this is certainly final We invested the night. I could see coyotes feet being the entranceway as they moved through the carport. Sometimes, you would bump the hinged door and it would open somewhat, and then be stopped because of the string holding it shut. It had been terrifying to see one of many crazy dogs' muzzles through the gap that is tiny they howled.

"Damn this old door." Granny slammed it again two more times before throwing a wood wedge it shut under it to help keep. The string jangled it shut as she fastened. Turning around, i really could see her look of fatigue give way to fury as she viewed the kitchen that is messy.

"Daniel Lee!" Grandpa hurried to his foot and ambled in, the screen home slamming behind him.

Today"Why didn't you are doing anything while I happened to be gone? This spot is a wreck!"

"i did so plenty whilst you had been gone, girl!"

"Oh, like the dishes?" She gestured to the sink that is overflowing of cups and dishes.

"I had to speed myself, and so I took out of the garbage, emptied the ash-trays, checked the mail, made some coffee…"

"And then sat around hearing music and watching the current weather channel."

"Don't be Granny this is certainly angry, I stated. "He has a bad back."

"I know sweetie." Granny sighed. "Why don't you and Kasey get outside and play?"

After-dinner, Granny took us into the industry aided by the oak tree. Kasey and I also utilized sticks we discovered like swords, slashing through the group that is periodic of lawn. You couldn't tell from the road, but trash littered the industry, smashed beer cans, worn-out garments, and just who understood what else. Kasey and I prodded at a sizable case this is certainly black ripping at the seams.

"Stay away from that, children! You don't know where it came from or what it really is," Granny said as she lit another smoke.

Kasey and I bolted down ahead, "fighting" other imaginary pirates until we came to the oak tree. We went under it, and swung through the low-hanging limbs around it, played tag. Kasey also assisted myself attain some acorns which can be stray a branch I couldn't attain. I was a little stressed, climbing. I were trying to get her kite from the spruce tree right in front garden once I smashed my arm last summertime, Kasey and. This thought eerily similar, but I got straight down without any trouble. We divided the acorns these people were doubloons between ourselves and pretended. Kasey could possibly be alright, in certain cases similar to this. Neither of us had siblings and it was fun some one this is certainly having play with. I experienced to admit, even if she had been awful occasionally, Kasey might be a lot nevertheless of fun.

"Eww," Kasey stated pointing between a couple associated with the tree's subjected roots. "What's that?"

"What is it Kasey?" Granny looked down through the clouds she was considering.

"It's moving," Kasey said, pointing.

A clump of ladybugs how big is a baseball crawled around and over top of each other. I couldn't think it absolutely was missed by us when we were playing our online game of label. I experienced no basic concept why these ladybugs were doing this. I wondered if Mrs. Smith would understand. She understood about lots of things.

"They should be huddling collectively to remain hot," Granny said. She had been switched by her mind up towards the darkening sky as thunder rumbled within the distance.

"Come on, you two. It sounds like rain is in the genuine method."

"Aww, Granny! Can't we stay a little longer? We're still looking for the X where in actuality the treasure is." Kasey pouted as she said this.

"Kasey," Granny said with an appearance that is stern her face.

"Come on, Johnny! Let's race back into the homely house."

"O.K." I ran since fast her, but it had been no use when I could after. Kasey was taller than me personally and a faster runner. I possibly could scarcely see her magenta jacket between your sporadic growths of grass and also the bush that is strange. Eventually, she was away from sight. I quit and attempted to get my breath. The rumble that is distant of became louder as I wandered all of those other in the past to your residence.

Granny made us simply take bathrooms before we visited the family area to look at television. We forgot to bring my sleepwear, so Granny gave me one of Kasey's ones which can be old wear. These people were flannel this is certainly red a zipper and built-in legs. Ky's pajamas were virtually identical, simply larger. Granny thought us wearing matching clothes would make a picture that is great. She clicked certainly one of us regarding the couch together with her polaroid. Granny had to get fully up early, with us long therefore she couldn't stay up.

"Don't stay up far too late." She stated, hugging us goodnight. Kasey got up and left the space. I decided getting among the VHS tapes prepared. The cartoon ended up being examined by me personally channels, but nothing great was on. I just started the "Speed Racer" tape when Kasey plopped straight down on the couch with a bowl of popcorn. We reached for a few whenever she jerked the bowl away from my reach.

"Don't wipe the hands-on my pajamas." She gestured to my lent ensemble.

"I wasn't likely to."

"Good. Because they're mine." I possibly could currently hear my grand-parents snoring in the home this is certainly small. I attempted to take pleasure from the cartoon, despite recognizing Kasey today had reign this is certainly no-cost torment myself just as much as she liked. She made fun of the way the people's lips did match exactly what they n't were saying. She mocked the figures and made myself want I had just visited sleep. Between her comments plus the wind that is howling i really could scarcely focus. We just completed one episode once I decided to go to sleep. I really could constantly use the tapes home and here enjoy all of them.

"At the very least she won't have the ability to bother me while I sleep," I thought.

I was incorrect. The overcast, rumbling heavens from earlier had offered solution to a thunderstorm. Lightning flashed contrary to the skeletal tree limbs out of the window and I also held Teddy tight. Kasey's long black hair hung from her upside-down head as she peered down through the bunk this is certainly top. Her face this is certainly pale looked myself in the dark.

"I bet you don't understand the witch that life in those woods." She pointed during the forests behind your house.

"There aren't any witches around here."

"Are therefore! Kathy Connors showed me personally a novel all about all of them at school."

"Goosebumps are only made-up stories."

"It wasn't a Goosebumps book, stupid. It was about a town nearby with a number of witches. They certainly were caught means that are casting making sacrifices when you look at the forests. These people were found because of the townspeople after reading the cries of kids they certainly were killing."

I did son't say everything. I just shuddered at the thought.

"Then," Kasey continued, "a couple of annoyed villagers chased all of them through the woods until they caught and executed every witch but one. She escaped and was seen traveling on her broomstick when you look at the sky night. She hovered over the gallows and said she would avenge the loss of the other witches in her own coven."

"Stop making things up. None of that's true." We shuddered.

"It is true. It absolutely was in that guide. It stated things that are bad to people just who tried acquiring her. Their plants did develop, their particular n't animals passed away, kids vanished without a trace. They never discovered her, and she nevertheless haunts the forests for this very time."

I held Teddy tight as thunder clapped and wind raged outside. I possibly couldn't watch for this visit to my grandparents to get rid of.

Wild birds spread from behind a bush even as we went through the industry that is bare. The thunderstorm associated with the past night had given method to a crisp, foggy morning. We discovered stick swords and made a decision to pick our game up of pirates from the night before. If we got through the overgrown fence line, however, our attention had been straight away redirected towards the oak tree. It had dropped. We viewed each other before tossing down our sticks and working to see what happened. Granny informed us the tree was over 200 years old, I really couldn't think it folded. I gasped for atmosphere when I attempted maintaining Kasey. With no tree sticking up in the heart of the field, I realized how effortlessly i really could wander off. Almost all of the tufts of lawn were bigger than I happened to be. Besides a trees which can be few the fence line, nothing else had been noticeable. Kasey ended up being no help. She went to date ahead i possibly could barely get a glimpse of her magenta jacked before she'd disappear completely behind the dense fog and foliage when I rounded a cluster of grass.

My lungs burned and my throat had been hoarse from breathing the cool atmosphere whenever we both ended during the picture this is certainly awful. The tree this is certainly once-great on the ground, its huge trunk splintered a couple of legs over the floor. A lot of the limbs were damaged or crushed down as they dropped. Kasey and I also looked over one another prior to getting closer. The cluster of ladybugs ended up being nowhere found. The limbs I swung from only yesterday lie shattered beneath the weight of this tree that is wrecked. Worse still, inside the stump this is certainly jagged I could start to see the lumber when you look at the center was lifeless. Frowning, I grabbed a small number of waterlogged, decomposing lumber. Just the outer few inches of the tree underneath the bark had been really alive. It absolutely was recognized by me was probably regarding the verge of failure since I very first saw it.

"You see," Kasey said, as I wiped the timber this is certainly rotten my arms. "It's the witch."

Kasey hopped up on the tree that is collapsed and wandered its size like a stability beam. "She's however haunting those woods. All those many years later, she's still making things which are bad."

I felt a chill, but couldn't tell if it came from Kasey's story or the snap this is certainly powerful appeared to come from nowhere.

"A witch couldn't have inked this," we said. "She'd be one hundred yrs . old chances are."

"Doesn't matter," Kasey jumped from the trunk. "Witches live hundreds of years on the bloodstream of young ones just like us."

I desperately wanted this is untrue. I tried to think of a genuine option to prove Kasey had been lying.

"The witch couldn't live all within the woods year. What about cold temperatures? She would have frozen to death."
Ads

"That's why she killed the farmer whom utilized to plant this area. The reason why don't you imagine anyone lives within the homely home in the crossroads?" Kasey gestured to the derelict house at the conclusion that is opposite of the field. A window from the house's turret peeked ominously through empty tree limbs and fog that is increasing.

"My dad said nobody lives here as it isn't safe. The roof was stated by him is caving in."

"Has he ever before already been there before?" Kasey wore a smirk that is bad her face.

"I don't…"

"Of course, he hasn't! Because the witch ended up being understood by him was living around." The wind was picking right up again, and I also felt cool standing next to the pine tree that's old.

"I'll bet none associated with grown-ups have gone to that particular house. They're most likely all scared, just like you."

"Am not!" I felt my eyebrow furrowing.

"Scaredy cat! Scaredy pet! Scaredy cat!"

"I am maybe not."

"Then include me."

"Where?"

"To the witch's house stupid." Before I could say everything, Kasey became popular through the fog. Her coat this is certainly bright very nearly vanished before I tried catching up along with her. I didn't desire to go to the homely home, but We definitely performedn't want to stay without any help within the fog. Only at that real point, I experienced no clue where Kasey ended up being. I simply knew the direction she went. The crow that is occasional from a hiding place round the clumps of grass as I struggled to steadfastly keep up. Their loud caws had been the sound this is certainly only could hear aside from the squishing of damp grass and my tense breathing when I went. The fog appeared to thicken by the end this is certainly far of field. In some locations, I possibly couldn't see more than a feet which are number of me.

I eventually achieved the tree line ahead of the house's lawn when I saw Kasey's magenta coat. She ended up being going slowly toward the porch that is back of the house. I ran the exact distance that is short catch up with her. She will need to have heard my footsteps with a finger to her lips because she looked to face me personally. She gestured for me personally to come closer.

"Somebody is in," She whispered.

"Stop telling lies." I shuddered in the idea. I thought revealed when you look at the fairly empty, albeit overgrown garden.

"I'm informing the reality." Kasey's eyes had been broad. "I saw a shadow move behind the upstairs window."

I viewed the home that is dilapidated understood it absolutely was in even worse form than I was thinking. Wooden siding hung loosely from the general edges of your home. Several of the windows were shattered. Vines from some plant this is certainly wild through the collapsed part of the roofing. The porch had been riddled with termite holes. The entranceway regarding the general straight back porch stood halfway available, offering us a view associated with the hallway. Wallpaper hung, peeling from chalky plaster. The floor this is certainly wooden covered with moss, scraps of report, and damaged ceiling tiles. The staircase had several broken tips. We stopped inside our tracks at the bottom for the porch tips.

"Come on, aren't you planning to come around?" Kasey seemed a lot less sure of by herself.

"Nobody could live in this location. Not really a witch."

"So, you state."

Kasey took the action this is certainly first the porch. I accompanied close behind, keeping an attention that is watchful the trees around the house. We thought as we advanced regarding the back-door like we weren't alone. I attempted considering some real method to get Kasey to go out of this spot once the porch creaked under our blended weight. We avoided the broken panels until we had been at the limit of the home that was destroyed. With an foot that is unsure, Kasey stepped in to the home. Stray pieces of glass crunched underfoot as I adopted from the carpet that is filthy. I looked through a doorframe to my right and could see light online streaming in through the holes in the roof. The vines I saw outside disappeared into a sink this is certainly huge with rotting leaves and blackened liquid. Dirt under my foot made more noise I today seen as a kitchen as I stepped in to the tiled floor of just what. The plaster from the walls left coarse dust that's white a lot of the counters and floors. I happened to be about to switch and discover Kasey once I stopped within my songs. There is a footprint this is certainly dirty the ground. We looked down in the mud this is certainly damp its sides and thought suddenly unwell. It was twice how big my personal foot. I implemented the outlines being muddy recognized they went within the stairs.

My eyes observed the stairs up to the landing and fixed themselves on a weathered door in the step this is certainly top. A door creaking echoed through the house. It originated from upstairs. Kasey went past me when you look at the hallway and out the door this is certainly right back. I heard noises like a cat hissing loudly as I bolted through the cooking area after Kasey. I believed my world spin as I slipped on some of the trash and strike the wood hall flooring with a thump that is loud. I clutched and gasped my upper body as I believed the wind knocked away from my lung area. Huge clumps of plaster ground loudly up against the timber and forgotten leaves of report crumbled as I scrambled out of the door that is front. A door someplace in the homely house slammed as I jumped through the porch. Kasey had been standing during the fencerow waving in my situation to perform. Her eyes seemed back scary. I looked to see a shadowy figure behind the curtain towards the top of the move that is turret.

We avoided the area the rest of the day. We didn't also keep the homely home, we simply remained from the sofa and out of the house windows until bedtime. That evening, Kasey left her blanket holding on the side of the bunk that is top cover the window considering our space, and found myself in the base bunk with me.

"I'll bet the witch saw us," Kasey stated.

"Maybe she performedn't." We knew just how foolhardy the suggestion had been before it had been said by me.

"Didn't you see her moving behind the upstairs curtain? She required seen us."

"Then why didn't she come after us? Clearly she wouldn't away why don't we get."

Kasey believed for a moment. I possibly could hear the flap, punch, flapping for the display that is worn-out in the carport. We reassured myself. We checked the relative back door before We stumbled on the bed. The chain was at destination. No person could open the hinged home from the exterior, not even with an integral.

"Maybe the witch just happens through the night. Like a vampire."

"Maybe." We set Teddy this is certainly truth be told there keeping tight. That i hadn't believed such a thing about witches morning. Now I was having a conversation this is certainly severe the likelihood you could be just over the barren area next to my grandparents' house.

"What are we planning to do?"

"I don't understand."

The wind billowed after dark screen close to the bunk-bed. I cringed as a branch that is reduced resistant to the glass. "I'll ignore it," I thought to myself. We wasn't going to let only a little wind bother me personally, maybe not whenever I had a problem this is certainly genuine.

That's when we heard the doorknob to your general straight back door rattle. I really could hear the noisy thumps as some thing slammed to the door this is certainly right back. We screamed in our beds since the sequence rattled with each try to shove the hinged door available. Maggie, the black colored lab barked and started growling in the door this is certainly straight back.

"Someone is wanting to obtain in!" Tears went down Kasey's face. The mattress could possibly be heard by myself within my grand-parents' room groan while they got up out of bed. With rate I wasn't accustomed to witnessing, Grandpa hurried after dark home that is available the visitor area together with his shotgun. The glow of this floodlights into the carport shined through the blanket covering our screen. Granny went into our space and tried her best to comfort us.

"Shhhh. It is alright," She said, hugging us. "It's just coyotes." The blanket dropped from the window in every the commotion. Now the as soon as familiar garden and fence line seemed menacing in the light that is blueish.

"Granny it's perhaps not coyotes. The witch is trying to obtain in!" Kasey cried once more.

"That old wives' story? Sweetie, there's nothing available to you but those dogs that are crazy. Grandpa is securing the hinged home, don't you worry."

"By lock, she implies shoving the wood wedge under the bottom to keep it sealed,as I seemed outside" I thought. I stared to the tree that is darkened and the area beyond. It absolutely was impractical to determine if everything was available to you, but my eyes kept tricks which could be playing me. Shoots of grass appeared to be a crouching witch. Empty tree limbs seemed like emaciated hands. Every rustling leaf and tree that's swaying me more uncertain about whether something lurked only beyond the reach for the floodlights outside.

We gathered adequate courage to venture away from the day that is next. The spruce this is certainly blue when you look at the breeze. I could nevertheless start to see the yellow splinters where I smashed a branch off trying to get my cousin's kite summertime this is certainly last. We remembered her informing me to head out regarding the limb alone for all of us both as it ended up being also tiny.

"We need in the future up with a strategy for just what to complete about the witch," Kasey said as she climbed in addition to the working platform for the well this is certainly old.

"Grandpa said not to play up truth be told there! The working platform is not safe to face on!"

Kasey grabbed the pump this is certainly long in the well and rocked on the balls of her foot. It creaked as she pumped water that is rusty the spout.

"But… Granny stated it had been just coyotes."

"She just wished to keep us from getting frightened. Can you wish two kids which can be bit know a witch ended up being trying to get into the household?"

I shook my mind. "No."

"Exactly. She most likely had no idea how to get reduce a witch in the first place."

I looked up at Kasey. "Do you?"

"Um," Kasey looked down as she jumped through the platform. "Salt! That's it. Witches can't get across a trail of sodium."

"How do you know that?"

"My cousin Jeremy said therefore. He's the main one which I'd like to borrow the written book about witches."

"I was thinking you stated Kathy Co…"

Kasey seemed furious. "Shut up. We said it's read by myself didn't I?"

"Yes." I looked down at my foot. "But just how are we planning to place salt right around the house? We'd require a massive bag!"

"Not when we simply perform some doors and windows. Here's what we'll do: We can wait till Grandpa and Granny tend to be asleep. Then, we'll go into the cabinet and acquire their particular might of salt. Then We can distribute the sodium. It is so easy!"

"But what in the event that witch gets us while we're outside?"

"She won't get us. Not whenever we complete ahead of the witching hour."

"The just what?"

"Midnight? That's when witches turn out."

Unexpectedly grandpa showed up in the porch. "Kids... Lunch is prepared."

Kasey and I trudged through the yard and returning to the house. Climbing the tips into the homely household, we noticed anything strange: the air was down. Grandpa may have turned down the volume during the day on till Granny got home while he saw the weather forecast and regional development, but he typically held it. The television has also been down even as we moved through the living room. If experienced incorrect for indeed there not to be some noise that is background the home. I pulled up a chair in the dining table and began crackers which can be crushing my chicken noodle soup. Grandpa ended up being quiet while he sat right down to eat. His typical, relaxed demeanor had been replaced with alert eyes and silence. He was using the drab that is olive from his military times and I could see brass and waxed paper cylinders in his pocket. We noticed these people were shotgun shells. Kasey and I also looked over one another once we consumed our soup. I wondered if she noticed this when law enforcement scanner screeched to life within the family room. Grandpa got up and turned the amount down following the dispatcher said some thing about a suspect being "at large". We wondered what that meant.

"Why aren't you enjoying music grandpa?"

He made a smile that is small. "i've a bit of a headache. It'll go away with a little peace."

We completed consuming and Grandpa requested us to keep inside while a phone ended up being created by him telephone call. I was thinking it absolutely was unusual as he ended up being chatting for him to use the call outside, but he stated we could watch TV. He talked in hushed tones as he paced the porch, periodically overlooking their shoulder. We wondered just what had him acting this genuine means as I fired up the television. Grandpa left it on the news and there was clearly a hand-drawn image of a guy with lengthy, scraggly tresses and strange-looking eyes. I did son't provide it much thought before switching to a cartoon station. Scooby-Doo was on and I constantly liked watching all of them solve mysteries. Another episode ended up being wished by me personally would be on next because Fred had been pulling a mask off a supposed "wolf-man". It had been constantly only a man in a mask. There were no beasts being real in spite of how real they appeared.

Kasey plopped down on the couch. "Just checked. There's plenty of sodium into the cupboard."

"Why can't we place the sodium down now? Within the daytime?"

You used all her spices on 'Experiments' this one time"Do you keep in mind exactly how mad Granny ended up being when? Besides, Granny might start to see the salt and try to clean it."

I felt embarrassed thinking back again to the time I dumped the spruce this is certainly entire into a blending dish. I was thinking a chemistry had been carried out by myself research, however in reality, I happened to be simply making a mess of nutmeg, cinnamon, and garlic powder.

"Are you sure it's safe?"

"Of course. We read that book. We also did a show-and-tell about this." We had been interrupted by the rattling associated with screen home.

"Well, Johnny," Grandpa stated. "Your parents are arriving straight back a early day. The escape ended, so they'll be here later or at the beginning of the early morning to pick you up tonight. They're regarding the genuine solution to the airport right now." He ruffled my hair as he stepped through the family area, lighting another tobacco cigarette.

"Your Granny is residence that is coming from work these days too. Maybe we'll have some more cheeseburgers for supper."

Grandpa smiled I could inform some thing had been off as he said these specific things, but. Kasey and I held TV this is certainly watching Granny got residence. Even with her back, the homely house ended up being quiet. She performedn't get onto Grandpa for not performing the laundry or clearing up at home. My grandparents stayed barely even spoke, except for several words which are whispered. My parents known as before they showed up while I happened to be in the bathtub to let my grandparents know these were on the way, nonetheless it is a couple of hours.

"We're planning to check out bed," Granny stated as she applied her eyes. "Johnny, your mother and father will probably be here late. tonight" She glanced in the time clock. "You and Kasey can view cartoons myself you'll wake me up if they get here until they arrive here, only promise. okay?"

"OK, Granny," we said, giving her hugs before Kasey and I settled back onto the settee.

"One more thing," Granny said from behind her room door. "Keep the doors locked."

I thought this a request this is certainly weird but Ky and I also both concurred. Granny visited sleep. I looked over the time clock nearby the TV. It was practically 11 o'clock. I wondered if I could get out of Kasey's idea that is crazy. It didn't take long before i possibly could hear my grandparents snoring in their room. I pretended to be enthusiastic about the film on TV. It was a kids' movie about witches attempting to capture a lady this is certainly little my age. She had a brother that is big was trying to keep her safe. "I wished my cousin was more like him," I was thinking as I saw Kasey vanish into the kitchen. I thought she was popcorn this is certainly making me hear the faint noise of a chair dragging across the floor to your cupboards. I thought as to what she was doing when the film abruptly had my complete interest. One of several small children in this film shook salt all around her just as the witches were closing in on her. Kasey hadn't found out about salt witches being maintained. She must have watched this motion picture and thought I'd never seen it. We felt betrayed. The feeling that is same had whilst the part associated with spruce tree cracked under my weight while I tried to have Kasey's kite. This was just another certainly one of Kasey's tricks.

She went back to the family room with a can picturing a girl keeping an umbrella.

"Here, you are taking this." She held out of the sodium shaker through the table. "Now, it is easy. We venture out the door that is front get round the left side, you are going all over right side, then…"

"No," I said. Kasey looked astonished. I do believe it had been one of the times being few ever confronted her.

"What?"

"I'm not likely to that side of the house. It's closest into the area that is bare the witch's household is."

"Yes, you will."

Me go right to the right side of the house, I'll get up Granny and tell her exactly what you're up to. "If you try to make" Kasey's lip quivered with disappointment.

"F-Fine," she said. "You take the side that is left you're such a fraidy-cat. You cover the windows in your corner for the homely house, and I'll cover mine." The sodium was thrown by her shaker at myself and waited next to the door. We viewed the time clock before she had been joined by me. We nevertheless had practically an full hour I was thinking, although I happened to be considerably less secure in this solution. I knew Kasey was only attempting to use myself again. I'd an idea when I put my sneakers on. Then just work until she had been out of sight, and then slip back inside like I became placing salt around the house windows. The entranceway towards the carport had that gap that is big it. I could spread salt under it in the house.

The door that is forward of house launched silently and Kasey gingerly closed the display screen door after us. "Meet straight back right here," she stated. I nodded as I climbed along the part this is certainly remaining of porch and salted across the screen on the front side of the house. The night that was cold made my breathing fog up as I held an eye fixed on Kasey. She already completed her window and disappeared around the corner of your home. When I was certain she wasn't finding its way back, I tip-toed up the porch and very carefully slipped within the display screen home. We banged down my footwear and moved towards the relative back door to distribute the salt onto the threshold. I felt significantly happy for standing up to Kasey. I tried to consider another correct time i had done this but couldn't.

The shaker ended up being nearly vacant while the top was taken by me off. I knelt to your ground to pour the past of my salt along the threshold. The white sodium shone in the light associated with the night that is clear. We admired the task I experienced done, even yet in the early morning if I was thinking it wasn't effective, and I also knew Granny wouldn't be happy whenever she found it. I happened to be planning to stand up when I froze. Under the door had been two boots that are dirty. I happened to be so surprised We didn't say any such thing before the door creaked open slightly, and I also saw the blade that is sharp of knife hook to the backlinks for the string holding the doorway sealed. I yelled for my grandpa when I knew the thing that was occurring.

I scrambled from the hinged door and underneath the dining table as I heard grandpa jump out of bed. Through the break regarding the hinged door, i really could write out unclear popular features of the guy outside as he shook the doorway violently, hoping to get in. The slim face, the wild, deranged eyes we knew it was the guy regarding the development section with the long hair. Grandpa ran to the home with absolutely nothing but their boxers plus the shotgun.

"Get the hell away!" He pumped the shotgun and also the supply with all the knife disappeared through the door this is certainly battered. Grandpa knelt straight down. "What happened? Will you be hurt?

Where's Kasey?"

We heard Kasey's scream that is high-pitched. Through the kitchen flooring, i possibly could see-through the window within the guest room. The man that is crazed run into Kasey looking to get away and grabbed her. Grandpa went out the trunk door with all the shotgun he couldn't move fast enough, maybe not together with bad straight back after them, but. The final I saw of my cousin had been her pale face screaming in scary and hand that is outstretched for grandpa as she disappeared to the overgrown field of Indiangrass beyond the get to associated with the floodlights.

You were held by every grave, their particular life, and their history. It reminds you it into the fullest, but is this correct that you have got only one shot at this life, and to live? We have skilled anything during my life that a lot of people haven't; it is so strange that even you aren't planning to think my experience.

My boyfriend of couple of years ended up being run over by an eighteen wheeler in the age of 21 years old. He ended up being home this is certainly coming work with his motorcycle while the truck motorist supposedly didn't see him until it absolutely was too late. His funeral was heavy, he'd plenty people being loved and none of them even surely got to state good-bye. It had been a closed casket funeral, and therefore I was never ever gonna see him again while he got put six feet under, I became saddened, certain.

Listed here a couple of weeks had been a blur. I had been stuck in circumstances this is certainly constant of and sadness, consuming myself to sleep and chain smoking cigarettes once I ended up being restless. Our love was therefore strong, it had been one you would read about in fairy stories. We had been meant for each other, we don't believe anyone could deny that, and that is why in my opinion he came ultimately back for me.

The night time he came back ended up being cool and stormy, wind whistled throughout out the house, that has been interrupted with all the rush this is certainly periodic of. We laid awake in my bed drinking on rum, and hearing the howls and splits from external, when abruptly a sound this is certainly brand new through my house. A knock on my door. The clock back at my nightstand reported I had crawled out of bed wondering who it can be that it was three each day.

I had crept down the stairs, heading towards the hinged door to obtain the response to my first concern. But just I noticed it absolutely was currently available as I surely got to the doorway! I gasped, wondering how the door have been exposed whenever I kept it locked at all hours associated with the evening! I ran to shut it, having to combat the wind to keep it close; I locked it and instantly heard a groan this is certainly soft from down the hallway. I had a wave this is certainly in short supply of, looking down to see dirty footprints proceeding towards the dreaded sound. I had understood during my head me to stick to the mossy, damp footsteps towards whoever or whatever it absolutely was that i ought to have only kept the house, but also for some explanation, my own body at the time had forced. We ended, maintaining my body hidden behind the wall surface, and switched my check out see what looked like a corpse!

The guy had been bony mangled, and rotten, most abundant in scent that is foul could previously imagine. Flesh peeled because the dirt slopped off onto my kitchen area flooring. We stared in surprise, when it had been understood by myself had been my boyfriend! He had come back! Rigor mortis crackled himself a glass of orange juice while he reached his half decayed hand up into the refrigerator, pouring. The juice poured into his mouth and then out of their throat appropriate onto the floor to the heap of mud and blood that is aged him. Quickly, he had turned around, just as if he was alerted of my presence. Nonetheless having already been frightened, we took cover behind the wall, nonetheless it did matter that is n't he saw me personally.

"Hi child, it's just me, you should not panic!" He said in a much more grungy and macabre means he had been alive than he had previously sounded whenever.

I had stood, just in full shock, wanting to grasp the thing that was occurring.

"That truck really did a number it doesn't matter because my love introduced me personally back! on myself, but" He proceeded.

We bolted along the hallway and to the door. At that brief minute, I understood it was impossible, I happened to be horrified!

"Baby, where have you been going?" He questioned, as he paced around the corner and along the hall towards me.

Their epidermis was peeling down, exposing much more bone than flesh, an opening in his throat showed juice that is tangerine dripping down, and his one attention ended up being covered with maggots along with other critters. We screamed, wanting to unlock the doorway.

"Baby, it's going to be okay, we are able to eventually permanently be together!!!" He shouted.

We eventually unlocked the door, however it, he approached myself, getting my face and offering me a beneficial long kiss back at my lips when I launched. Ab muscles kiss that is exact same had missed since his absence.

"I like you," He told me.

We beamed, offering him another kiss.

Just one more time

Stacey Chapman pulled difficult in the steel this is certainly cold of gate. The rusted iron hinges resisted and it also squealed as it moved. She winced at the noise since it slashed through the peaceful of the cemetery. She pulled difficult once more. It moved another six inches but would more go no. She glanced around to ensure she hadn't attracted any company that is undesired then checked her watch. Twelve minutes until midnight. She nevertheless had time.

She modified her glasses, tied back her long, brown tresses, after which slipped through the gate that is antiquated. The moonlight illuminated the mausoleum up ahead. The dwelling this is certainly old with dried out, lifeless vines engulfing it, as though unwilling to discharge their particular prize. They snaked their way around grey weathered rock because old as the woods surrounding it. Two ornate pillars fought to carry the stonework up as it slumped aided by the body weight of the century-long burden.

She edged closer through the lawn this is certainly lengthy weeds. The pockmarked wall surface that is external of construction ended up being covered in many years of mold and moist. The rock that is motionless that hung above the two huge, black wooden doorways sneered down, warning off anyone foolish adequate to try and enter. That's me personally, she believed as she crept ahead, stupid, stupid, stupid. She could only make the name out above the doorways, created into a worn, granite plaque

MARCOVELLE

She believed uneasy seeing that name. Everybody in the city understood it together with legend it bore. Vincenzo Marcovelle—the Monster of Milford. He was a young child killer, murdering three of their four daughters being younger a hand sickle back in 1913. She heard that whenever the authorities stormed Vincenzo's home they discovered the bloodied bodies of his kiddies outlined on to the floor, their hands entered over their chest with one white rose in each hand that is little. Vincenzo ended up being there, clenching the blood-soaked sickle while he calmly rocked straight back and" that are forth saying one more," repeatedly.

He would never get a chance to finish his grizzly task. Vincenzo's test was fast. He was found bad and two days later delivered to the chair that is electric.

Stacey shivered whenever she pictured it. There was in fact one empty spot-on the ground your day they took him away, empty salvage for a single rose that is white. The area intended for the child that is fourth Mary, Stacey's great-grandmother. Mary was indeed away at the physician along with her mama that and much to Stacey's relief, was in fact spared day.

Stacey had discovered the relationship by accident the before, when searching through a stack of genealogy papers disseminate on the kitchen table day. A spare time activity that is present of father's, he had tracked their family tree all the way back to its beginnings in Europe and discovered the connection into the Marcovelle range. Her close friends Cory and Trina had a field when she told all of them day.

"Holy shit, Stacey. You're related to the Monster?" Cory said eyes broad with glee. That they had met due to the Marcovelle legend. They certainly were assigned becoming partners for a presentation in English. It was wanted by her becoming about songs, but Cory had insisted it be about the Marcovelle family members. It didn't take him long to generate the fundamental idea of Stacey using a midnight selfie together with her great-great grandfather.

"It will be so lit! The household reunion that is creepiest ever." Cory had stated.

"Come on, Stacey, you should do it." Trina included. "Of course, then just— if you're also scared"

"I'm not afraid!" Stacey clicked straight back.

Of course she had beenn't—at least not of Vincenzo's ghost. She just wasn't therefore sure about anyone else that could be loitering in graveyards in the exact middle of the evening.

As Stacey achieved the mausoleum doorways, she felt just as if she were being viewed. She seemed around, fearful. She couldn't see much through the darkness but the obscure shapes of gravestones and some trees which are squat. She wondered if her friends had followed her.

"Cory, is she asked the darkness, "Trina? which you?"" She waited for an answer, but the remained still night. She decided to guarantee. "Hey, Cory, Trina says she really wants to hook up we shared with her you liked males. with you but" There had been still no effect. Satisfied that her friends weren't spying she turned back towards the home on her behalf.

She cleared away a brittle that is few and then ended as she noticed the rusted sequence and padlock lying on the ground. She reached out to grasp the lock and wasn't astonished to locate that it twisted freely in her hand. The cemetery had been a spot this is certainly popular vagrants and medication people. Tonight she hoped there have been none in residence.

Turning back to the hinged doors she offered them a push with both-hands. They performedn't budge. So she braced her neck as she could against them and pushed since hard. The doorway scraped and screeched across the surface until it absolutely was open simply adequate on her behalf to fit by. Tilting her head in through the orifice she ended up being attacked because of the smell of urine and another old, musty fragrance she couldn't destination. "Ugh, gross!" she said. Disgusted, she ended up being taken by her mobile phone out of her back pocket and entered.

I'm appropriate away from mausoleum. May I just take a pic associated with the front doorways? It smells totally disgusting in there.

She waited a brief moment for Trina's response. It was encouraging this is certainly n't.

Nope! The dare is 4 u to simply take a selfie inside the mausoleum right at midnight. Say hi to Vincenzo in my situation!

She entered straight back, Screw you, believed for a second, and then included a face that is smiley for good measure.

She imagined at once your family must have already been rich having their burial that is own crypt. The legend was that Vincenzo wasn't also buried truth be told there initially. Due to his crimes, he was hidden in an grave that is unmarked upstate, only a year later his body ended up being exhumed due to reported paranormal 'disturbances' within the cemetery that contained their stays. The authorities didn't think any one of it needless to say, nevertheless the burial-ground began to get condition that is cult spiritual excitement hunters. They might appear in droves, hoping to get a glimpse of the Monster of Milford. It had been enough to convince them to maneuver Vincenzo to the grouped family mausoleum.

Stacey put her phone into flashlight mode and presented it in the front of her, then, crinkling her nostrils resistant to the odor, she stuck her mind through the hinged door once more.

"Hello? Is there any person here?" The darkness had been expected by her, with no response. "If there's any rapists or murderers in here personally i think it's fair to warn you that I'm pretty scrappy, therefore don't try anything, OK?" She smiled a nervous smile that is half slipped through.

For an instant she believed anything grab the base of her jean shorts and panicked. She swung her fist down and behind going to anyone who had grabbed her and struck one thing razor-sharp. Sobbing out in pain, she looked down and saw that her short pants were caught on an errant nail sticking from the woodwork.

"Dammit," she cursed, much more from concern than discomfort. a scratch this is certainly long throughout the heel of her hand already beading with blood. Swearing once again, she wiped her hand on the hoodie and reached right down to remove her shorts through the nail, then pressed the rest of the real means through the entranceway.

She took a couple of actions inside then played and stopped her light around. The inner appeared as if one thing away from an horror film this is certainly old. Big, round arches undulated across the space on whose walls hung steel this is certainly classic. In the past they'd have held torches but now contained long-neglected lanterns blanketed in a layer this is certainly thick of. Given that light swept through the available area, it brushed over rows of storage space niches that presented the ashes associated with the dead. Over each one of these sat a brass nameplate. Many had been covered in a rough film—Benjamin that is green Antonio, Samuel, Desmond—the names proceeded in rows across the inside.

She moved up to one archway that included only three plaques. As she read: Ruth Marcovelle, Constance Marcovelle and Lucy Marcovelle as her light illuminated every one she believed a chill. Right here had been the stays associated with the three women that Vincenzo had murdered dozens of complete years back. She thought an abrupt pang of sadness at just how innocent these young girls have been, and just how these people were betrayed therefore very because of the guy this is certainly very needs to have safeguarded all of them. Trying, she touched the cool metal of each and every plaque in turn, saying a prayer this is certainly hushed. She lingered a brief moment much more then turned away.

Her base struck something that went clattering over the stone floor. Startled, Stacey shone the light in direction of the sound locate an alcohol that is vacant resting contrary to the side of a sizable construction at the center for the space. Gradually raising her light from the flooring, she could make completely a large, marble sarcophagus. She cautiously relocated up to it and ran one-hand on the surface that is smooth of stone, her hands making a trail in the dense level of dust. The tomb it self had been unremarkable. The slab that is rectangular featureless with the exception of just one term carved into the marble in strong letters:

VINCENZO

So here he was, the kid this is certainly infamous himself. She stared during the tomb as well as for a moment she could visualize the Monster of Milford throwing the slab apart and rising up with bleached bones and dry, papery skin, reaching on her to participate him in his endless rest. She discrete a laugh that is nervous.

"OK Vince, I hope you're not camera-shy,as she turned-off the flashlight then put the camera app to selfie" she stated. Turning her back regarding the tomb the device happened by her call at front of her. She could start to see the sarcophagus it in the shot behind her and lined. She believed for a second, then held within the middle hand of her left-hand as a present this is certainly special Trina.

She ended up being going to drive the image switch whenever one thing relocated behind her in the display screen. She ended up being certain of it. A grey mass that is shadowy from left to right in the area between her and also the sarcophagus. Turning to look, her eyes darting forward and backward, she pointed the light in the direction that is same could see absolutely nothing except the rows of burial markets coating the wall surface behind her. She swallowed, then licked her mouth. Most likely some animal, she thought, maybe not totally convinced.

Stacey lifted the device yet again, now attempting to be done aided by the thing that is entire. Her hand trembled as she snapped the photo. The flash strobed a times which are few stopped. Lifting her hands to rub her eyes, she cursed. "Dammit! Good job Stacey." She could see nothing but a mass of bobbing dots that are white. She blinked a times that are few tapped on her discussion with Trina, quickly attached the photo and delivered it. Nonetheless wanting to blink away the dots, the device was held by her out in front side of her like a flashlight and began to go.

It buzzed before she'd taken a lot more than a couple of tips.

LOL work that is good! Nonetheless it doesn't count

She lifted one eyebrow and entered straight back. What are you speaking about? Why doesn't it count?

The deal ended up being it alone for you to do. You cheated.

"Huh?" she said, then typed, I WILL BE alone! Neither of you'd adequate guts to get this done beside me remember?

She could begin to see the doors which are big the other end for the room and switched toward all of them. She got about four steps whenever her phone started to vibrate. Trina ended up being calling her.

"What would you like, Trina? This really isn't the full time that is most readily useful."

"Get out of here today, Stacey."She seemed stressed.

"What do you consider I'm trying to accomplish? Did you think we planned to here camp out?"

"Stacey, seriously, there's someone else in there to you. Only move out today!"

"Stop it Trina! It is creepy enough in this accepted spot without you wanting to frighten myself. End being a shithead!"

"Stacey, I indicate it! Look at the picture. There's anything—"

She hung up, Trina could possibly be such a jerk. She could see Cory pulling a stunt like this but maybe not her.

"There's someone in there with you!" Stacey said in a mocking, high-pitched vocals. She chuckled, but she had been sensed by her heartrate speeding up. She hadn't looked at the photo before sending it, the good news is she thought a sickness rising from the base of her belly as a finger this is certainly shaking over the screen and tapped the message that included the picture.

The image went to dimensions this is certainly full and exactly what she saw there drained the bloodstream from her face and left her tongue sensation like sandpaper.

She was in the foreground with Vincenzo's tomb it had been a figure behind her, but standing about a base off to the right of. She ended up beingn't yes it had been big and it had one dark, hand resting on the tomb if it had been man or woman but. It is facial features had been distorted in a wash of grey and black but it's eyes had been like deep, black pits. The figure's other side looked become holding something with a handle that ended in a curve this is certainly long. It appeared to be some type of knife.

It appeared as if a sickle.

Stacey could feel adrenaline coursing through her as a sound that sounded such as the crunch of dry, dead leaves hissed in her own ear.

"Mary"

The shout that came she had made before from her had been like no sound. The telephone dropped from her hand and immediately the readily available space was cloaked in blackness. She ran, charging headlong into the darkness, perhaps not caring the thing that was in front of her.

She handled only seven strides before slamming face initially into one of several walls.

Disoriented, she shook her head and organized a tactile hand to her nostrils. She tasted the blood as it went down her lip. She no longer had any fundamental concept where the door was. For a second she thought it had vanished—that whatever was at only at its leisure with her had sealed her in forever so that it could eliminate her. Then, she saw a thin strip of light in the darkness forward as she twisted her head around in anxiety. It wasn't far and relief flooded through her.

Thank God, she believed, thank God, thank God, thank God.

Then she had been falling.

One thing pushed her difficult on her as well as she went sprawling ahead, her ankle twisting. Simple ended up being heard by her as she hit the marble floor. The pain sensation had been agonizing and she cried out. Rolling over onto her back, she gripped her knee to her upper body.

"No!" she pleaded to your darkness, tears blurring her sight, "I'm sorry! Kindly! I'll go...I'll leave right now, just please don't hurt me." The crypt stayed hushed as a result. Her ankle throbbed but her fear won out of the pain and she attempted to push herself up. She performedn't get far before something shoved her back once again. This time around, the force performedn't disappear completely, just as if a body that is hefty sitting on her behalf. She next believed one thing press that is cool her throat and knew it was Vincenzo's sickle. Then your respiration returned—that dry, dead inhaling and exhaling appropriate beside her ear.

"Just yet another."

The vocals sounded want it came from inside her mind. She could hear the satisfaction into the thing's words at finally getting just what it had so longed for—the last of an bloodline this is certainly unbroken.

Stacey had not been planning to die in this location that is terrible. She heaved with both her hands to up lever by herself, but the more she tried, the greater pressure the apparition placed on her body. She could feel the blade that is frigid in to the side of her neck. She tried to kick her legs however the stress on her chest ended up being way too much and she ended up being quickly running away from air. Dots popped and danced in the front of her eyes. Desperately, she flailed her hands out looking for anything, something that could help her. She begun to damage. She tried to scream once more but absolutely nothing arrived.

Then, her hand that's right hit. She saw a small, blinking light that is orange the black. Her cellular phone! She snatched it up and hit thoughtlessly at where she believed the pinnacle that is thing's. She struck one thing solid and heard a crunch that is gratifying. The respiration this is certainly bad into a pain -filled hiss as well as the pressure on her body vanished. She gasped and coughed for atmosphere, then tried to remain.

Her ankle that is broken would help her weight and she fell back off, falling her phone again. She crawled the past legs which are few the entranceway, sobbing uncontrollably. She put her hand from the edge of the frame and pulled herself to the strip this is certainly slim of the released through the orifice. Once more the sound this is certainly monstrous within the chamber, louder this time around.

"MARY"

She thrust madly for the light beyond your mausoleum however something grabbed the relative straight back of her hair. She screamed and thrashed, but her tresses would come free n't.

Panicking she achieved back once again to fight the entity off but considered sharp steel instead. Her eyes exposed large in realization. It absolutely was the nail that is exact same had caught on her behalf shorts in route in. She rapidly grabbed a wad this is certainly tight of locks only in front of the nail and pulled because hard as she could. There clearly was a ripping noise into a kneeling place and scrambled from the mausoleum because it tore no-cost, then with rips and snot running down her face she achieved out and grabbed a small number of weeds, pulled herself.

She wanted to remain and run but her ankle wouldn't allow her, so she crawled as quickly as she could over the grass this is certainly dew-soaked. Stacey didn't know if the fact had been she didn't care behind her or not but. She only desired to get a long way away out of this location this is certainly terrible the nightmare it contained.

Then a tactile hand grabbed her leg.

She banged and shrieked furiously however the entity ended up being also powerful therefore the discomfort in her ankle ended up being also great. Her nails clawed the floor to buy her back across the wet ground because it pulled. She looked around in desperation for something that she could use as a weapon but there is absolutely nothing but the grass that is cool.

a body weight satisfied on her as well as an hand that is unseen her head back. The thing that is last Chapman heard as the cool material for the blade slid across her throat ended up being three whispered words.

"Just one more time"

The boy strode rapidly along the dust roadway. The around him was peaceful night. He tore down their black gown all over old hand sickle as he moved holding it away in order to not get bloodstains on their clothing, and wrapped it. He smiled, recalling what if experienced like if the blade sunk into her flesh. Like anything ended up being full.

It felt great.

It absolutely was wished by him didn't need to be Stacey, but she was just what the Monster required—the end of the bloodline. It must be her.

Cory stepped a quick way to the woods beside the roadway, dug a hole together with his arms and dropped in the gown this is certainly bloody. He had been evaluating up whether or not to bury the sickle also or throw it in to the quarry on their way residence when his phone buzzed.

Cory! Answer the telephone! I however can't get through to Stacey. Where r u?

He looked at Trina's message, then at the sickle lying when you look at the dirt.

Just one single more.

Heathenberry Forest's Wishing Well

a rock was tossed by myself along the well. It clattered resistant to the walls as it bounced in one part to some other. I waited, straining both ears. No sign that the bottom was indeed reached by it.

"Hello?" We whispered tentatively in a decreased sound this is certainly shaky We peered on to the darkness, my eyes not able to penetrate its inky depth. My voice ended up being reverberating up against the sodden ancient walls, lessened to a choir that is discordant of this was harassing the stillness regarding the enclosed darkness within. Anything felt down. I happened to be maybe not said to be here. It had taken on all the night for me to collect my courage up which will make my way across the barren land alone before going into the Heathenberry Forest. Jamie Coldon's terms was in fact echoing in my mind all the real method to the clearing.

"If one thing answers you, just be sure you don't tell it your title,as we moved throughout the side of the forest adjacent to an old dilapidated train tunnel due North" he had cautioned me personally the day prior to.

"Why not?" He'd been expected by me personally. "And what is going to respond to me?"

He previously been looking at the summertime that is reddening, his pale-blue eyes sparkling with mischief and entertainment.

"You ask also questions being many child. Stupid questions. Just don't fucking get it done, alright? Very few men and women know where to find that stinkin' well that is old. Each goes indeed there becoming informed if they are going to be successful or otherwise not inside their everyday lives. You toss a dime over for every question. Make it quick. Never ask questions whose response you don't wish to know. Most importantly, never ever tell it your title! Or it's going to away steal your soul."

I experienced gasped and cringed I had never heard any child my age usage that sort of harsh language before at him because. But Jamie had been one to work cool and avove the age of their age that is actual for. Besides, he had been much older than I happened to be.

"You're kidding, right, Jamie?"

"The only reason why i will be here speaking with at this point you, is really because personally i think sorry for you personally. Your parent had been a person this is certainly great. He assisted my children a great deal. I'm perhaps not doing this for you personally, cretin! Kathy and I also leaves for the city week that is next. Don't tell anybody you had been told by me that! We've got everything identified already. Her buddy has a accepted location for us somewhere. We're getting married as soon as we leave this village this is certainly stinkin. We're perhaps not coming back. Her father will surface me live myself again after running away with his only child. if he ever before sees"

His pale face that is round been contorted into a combination of dedication, hope, but additionally anguish as he carried on.

"If you're wise, you receive out of this location just you drop your mind as well as you can prior to. This type of person hopeless. Or go to that really. Whatever. If that enables you to happy. I don't care. Hold back until the clock strikes midnight. Make no body that is sure you or knows where you're going. You have to do it alone. Or else you won't be answered because of it. That mountain is seen by you over there?" He pointed to your west at a dark slope that is bluish within the plain in the length. "There is a trail this is certainly small top from it. Follow it. It shall lead you due south in to the woodland. Because the bush grows thicker through it, you'll arrive at a little clearing in the center of the woodland where you can weave easily through the woods that one may scarcely smash. That's where the fine is. Don't proceed with the path West beyond the clearing. There's marshes. Men and women have died and drowned trying to make their particular means across the godforsaken plain."

And he had been appropriate. Air had been chilly when I appeared from the treeline. I experienced found myself walking at a tiny clearing that is about circular had been devoid of something bigger than knee-high dandelions. And there in the exact middle of the mini savanna, very nearly hidden into the darkness from probing eyes, I'd seen a little rock that is dilapidated, its construction black colored and sunken.

"Hello?" We called on once again louder but still as reluctant, my face this is certainly whole tensed. This time around a silence this is certainly terrible filling the fine. There were no echoes, as though the well had simply swallowed my sound entire. Perplexed, I bent right down to select another stone from the floor.

"Hello?" a voice instantly rose. I gasped in horror and cringed away simply to trip over my legs which are own. I fell backward and landed hard back at my buttocks. Himself was going to rear up from his subterranean tomb to get me, one thing flashed across my head as I sat there within the cool hard floor and waited, experiencing believing that the devil. A cautionary story Jamie had told me previous today he previously already been employed by many years before he left for the apple farm where.

"You dare to summon it, you have to there finish your organization. Remember to say many thanks and goodbye when you're done, usually it can think you're maybe not done and follow you around, viewing you when you look at the shadows wherever you go."

I struggled to rise to my legs and stood gazing intensely during the derelict stone mound, frowning at the signs being ancient-looking into its rough surface. My upper body ended up being heaving quickly with anxiety and anxiety. That sound had stimulated something I had never understood I had in me personally that. This worry this is certainly primal of unknown. Of exactly what awaited beyond the darkness.

"Hh-hello?" I chirped.

"Hel-lo …," it drawled with a sound that is contemptuous advised disguised danger. It sounded cozy but additionally remote at the time this is certainly same. There clearly was an tone that is unnervingly familiar it I noticed. It very nearly seemed like my voice that is own distorted, further and feline-like.

"Don't be afraid. Come closer …," it hissed almost inaudibly.

"What … what exactly are you?" I stammered.

"Well … I'm a wood-fairy." It discrete a chuckle this is certainly gleeful.

An image of tiny winged-human with pointed ears and delicate functions drafted through my head immediately, which would not match the sound this is certainly destructive below.

"Really?"

"Yessss …," it hissed loudly, as though blowing environment through gritted teeth. "You see those symbols? They've been called Ogham Inscriptions, an magic this is certainly old to keep myself right here. I will neither hurt nor touch you, regardless if I wanted to."

"I … I need your assistance. Can I have always been assisted by you?" I became afraid of engaging myself much more with this being that is disembodied but I knew it absolutely was the only way in my situation. Nothing else works.

"What is it?"

"I miss my father." I started initially to sob. My shoulder shook vigorously as I rested my face down from the cold stone this is certainly rugged, feeling hopeless and defeated. And incredibly soon I became overrun with a sense of outrage and indignation once more. I was not attention that is having to pay my surroundings. The woodland around me had fallen quiet. The psithurism of this woods within the wind had ceased out of the blue, as though the land this is certainly entire holding its breath in expectation.

"Understanding it?" it asked once more. Colder and more demanding.

I lifted my face-off the stone and stared in to the darkness under, experiencing slightly confused. On myself, disintegrating into shadowy walls that have been pushing me incrementally from all directions towards the inky depth, to resolve to the call of the void as I narrowed my eyes to concentrate on wanting to capture a glimpse associated with the slightest motion, we felt such as the woodland was closing in.

"Hello?" I leaned on the mound and arched my body to peer down.

"Tell me, what-is-it?"

"What d—"

"What do you want me to do?"

We launched my lips but could not find the expressed terms to express. I retreated thinking perhaps it had been perhaps not a idea that is great. Perhaps I should only immediately go homeward rather than come back to this blasted heath.

"You can let me know. What is it you would like? You will be helped by me," it said coyly.

"Can you bring him back once again to me personally?" The text had escaped my mouth before i possibly could even stop myself.

There were a couple of seconds of silence that almost made me switch on my heels and lose, not planning to hear any longer of what it had to say. It thought so wrong speaking with some thing you could not see as it was hiding at nighttime, the embodiment of darkness it self. I toyed aided by the basic concept of what was genuine and what was maybe not. But also then, I knew that I was trespassing the border of truth.

"Of course," it said.

"R-rreally?" I asked.

"Would you believe me your dad ended up being down right here beside me, looking up at you if we said? And all sorts of you had to complete was jump over becoming with him."

"Uhm, I don't believe that's a good idea." A step ended up being taken by myself out of the well, rubbing at my face. For starters, I knew exactly where my father was. Six legs under the ground at Roccocherry Cemetery various kilometers due west through the borders of city where we had had him interred a few weeks before, not in the base of an old fine this is certainly dilapidated. The idea of death ended up being one thing I was however struggling to get a grasp on. For many we knew he might be elsewhere as well, waiting. I happened to be just a young kid and there was clearly only a hint of doubt flashing across my ideas when I considered its terms. Will the autumn is survived by me once I can't even start to see the base? Can it be informing me the facts?

a cool laugh that is high-pitched from here, devoid of any feeling. It seemed hollow and insincere.

"You're one wise kid."

"So, could you really ..." I hesitated.

"Yesss. I shall deliver your dad back. Can it make you thrilled to again see him? Clearly it shall."

"What ... what's the catch then?" He was asked by me personally cautiously. "What would you like from me personally?"

"Very bold of one to believe i would like anything at all away from you."

"Then ... what—"

"Understanding your name, dear?"

We unsealed my lips to resolve but then Jamie's words the before flashed across my head once again day.

You my title" I am not allowed to tell"

"Why, given that's a lie. Just who told you that?"

"My buddy."

"Well, just what do we know concerning this friend this is certainly funny of? Isn't he since huge and slow as a bovine this is certainly grazing a summer day?"

"Everyone understands the principles. You can't learn by us our brands."

"Well every person doesn't desire to deliver their parent straight back from the dead, now do they? However you do. You've been lacking him a total lot, have actuallyn't you? Also it's killing you. This really is a very favor this is certainly huge ask of me personally. Besides, I only want to be your friend. Aren't pals likely to know one another's title? Or at the very least we could remain on a basis this is certainly last-name that is far more convenient for you."

"Isn't there other method th—"

"Oh yes. There is."

"What is it? Kindly tell me!"

"i would like human sacrifice. Bloodstream."

"W-wwhat … performed you just say? Bb-blood? Real human blood?"

It burst into fun that is mirthless sounded unpleasant and cool.

"Wouldn't it be less difficult myself your name, my dear son? if you just told"

Then I decided it to simply opt for it that it will be well worth. All I had to accomplish was inform it my name and my dad would go back to me. It had been maybe not rocket science. We exposed my mouth but whatever instinct had held me personally from performing this for the last twenty moments or more, suddenly caught up if you ask me again.

"Yes, friend? Your title. Tell me your name," it said reassuringly. "And you and your father that is dear will reunited. That's all it can take."

It took a billed energy of might to break my silence. But between heaving breaths and teeth which are gritted we eventually relented. It absolutely was the point that is right do. That evening, I stumbled on the truth about Heathenberry Forest myself of things beyond my understanding since it talked to.

***

Katherine Deanshaw's eyes had been puffy and red when I saw her the afternoon that is after the town. She seemed unhinged and troubled. She was searching during my course for the minute that is briefest in such a way just as if wanting to ask me personally one thing, which under different conditions, if perhaps things was in fact different, i might being over happy to tend to. She had for ages been a girl that is good. She waved for her becoming involved at me personally and beamed confusedly, then walked away with John Clearwater, the boy of this richest guy into the village with whom her father had always longed. It pained us to not be able to help her. It genuinely performed.

But I had a need to disengage myself from any obligation that has been not my own. I experienced already been anticipating things that are subsequently witnessing into location; My father's return. It was the matter that is mattered in my experience. I happened to be just fourteen after all.

We live alone in a apartment that is one-bedroom. Therefore can anyone tell me the reason why there clearly was a lady sitting on my settee TV that is watching?

I became in my room getting some work done whenever I had gotten a little hungry and planned on walking to the home getting some leftover meals that is Chinese. My kitchen sits next to the family room, and also as soon I noticed the tv screen had been on when I stepped in to the dark hall. I understand We never ever ended to watch something onto it, which means this was a sudden banner that is red.

Thinking that maybe it absolutely was upgrading or possibly Alexa had switched it on in error, we wandered up to turn it down, but my heart dropped whenever I saw a woman with oily hair this is certainly black on my couch watching it. For an instant, I was perplexed I walked in, and I also knew all the doors and windows were closed because we understood there clearly was no one right here whenever. From the right time I came home, I hadn't heard anybody break in, how the hell could people be sitting there? Following the confusion passed away, I wanted to stroll forward and have exactly what the hell she had been performing within my home, but something screamed that that could be a blunder this is certainly grave. That's what the impression was like if anybody has ever skilled sleep paralysis. I told my body to maneuver, nevertheless the part that is primal of brain declined vehemently. I gradually crept straight back inside my space and simply waited in silence.

At this stage I'm sure you're currently screaming me personally, I wanted at us to call the cops and trust to! Absolutely nothing at that time would've made me feel much better than to possess one or two armed cops truth be told there to deal that I didn't need along with her therefore. But if I'm being truthful? I didn't want her to listen to me speaking. We felt like that'd be a nightmare if she had walked to my area, I'd be caught, and also at that minute.

We got the courage to realize that is least and see just what she was as much as after waiting for half an hour in quiet.Pushing myself up, we cracked the door open just enough to obtain a view this is certainly away from hallway and appearance at where she was sitting.If I didn't know any better, I'd have assumed she'd just gotten into the wrong house and was relaxing like any other regular person. But everything was possible... Down.

It nearly looked just as if she was slumped forward from the settee. Part of me wanted to believe she was sleeping, but what happened next shattered that illusion. She reached a arm this is certainly disgustingly very long the doorway and unlocked it from her seated position with convenience. I haven't measured yet, but eyeballing the distance from my chair towards the home, it had to be at least 8 or 9 legs away from the end this is certainly low.

She slowly stood up and made an energy this is certainly clumsy walk towards it. Her human body was... Horrifying. She had been... Tall. Uncomfortably so. I'd say she was maybe over 9 feet with hands that touched the floor and pulled behind her if I'd to guess. Her fingers each sported roughly 11 hands which had to every be around a foot in total. From what I keep in mind, she was completely naked with drooping skin that hung loosely off of her severely body that is slim. She was also paler than I thought possible. Her epidermis showed up virtually grey, and i'd believe her skin belonged to this of someone recently deceased if I didn't understand any benefit.

She didn't move gracefully. She dragged her human body that is massive towards home and lifted her long arm to the doorknob to pull it open. It virtually looked like she had to break her bones which are very own complete the action. But she ended as she pulled the doorway available and relocated a spindly leg outside. My blood ran cool because she slowly switched her head I caught a glimpse of her face towards me, and. I desired to scream when I didn't see any eyes. Simply a exterior that is puffy drooping eye holes and a mouth with long rubbery lips that drooped past her shoulders in a permanent appearance of anguish.

I did son't know if she even had the capacity to if she saw me or. All we remember was her turning her head back outside and leaving my house. She shut the doorway than it ever before did behind her, and I also ended up being left in silence with my heart pumping faster. We rushed outside with my phone to see on video clip, and I... I wish I hadn't if i really could catch her. If only I had only shut the door and gone to fall asleep or gotten intoxicated and attempted to pass your whole thing off as a fucked up nightmare, but what We saw wasit had been real... I'm sure.

We seemed outside in the cool black, and I also saw her dangling off the region of the building like a spider that is fucking. The screen of the person above myself had been open. She was fishing around, and after a matter of seconds of researching, she pulled away their boy. Her hand had been entirely wrapped around the mind, and I also couldn't inform she slinked down to the darkness utilizing the youthful man when they were alive or dead by the time.

It had been caught by me all on video. I must've watched that video a hundred times before deleting it. I am talking about, just what the fuck was We supposed to do with it? Do you believe law enforcement would believe it is a piece that is real? Also they are doing when they did just what the hell could? And as a parent, are you currently better off thinking that your kid ran away or understanding that we can't even commence to comprehend it was taken by an entity?

At the least with the previous, you've got hope that perhaps you'll see all of them once more. I recently couldn't bring myself to create up such a concept that is crazy a grieving family. Or worse. Have them trust in me and go searching for something that no one should try to get a hold of ever. I knew as long it, I'd be tempted to look at it, and each time I watched it, I'd be driven further into insanity when I held.

There have been more stories of children lacking as of late. I've even heard some rumors about animals going missing from people's houses. Interestingly adequate, I even heard a story about a guy disappearing this is certainly full-grown. He had been never ever seen again with simply no trace of where he went or the reason why he left. The one and only thing suggesting any type of outside power ended up being an window this is certainly available, and some strands of hair authorities couldn't match any DNA to.

It has taken rather a cost back at my life. I attempted to locate informative data on this plain thing, but as far as I understand, there's nothing. If anyone around has already established a experience this is certainly similar please inform your story or share images of the thing when you have them. I recently want to know I'm perhaps not crazy. I'm stopping my work and sticking to my brother on the other side for the country the next day. There's no way that is fucking sticking around that thing more than i must.

We don't intend on becoming here considerably longer, but evening this is certainly last heard a knocking within my home. I understand the time that is next see it; We won't be telling a tale afterwards. But I also know, I'm burning this damn that is whole straight down beside me.

Have you ever heard the thought of nature guides or protectors which can be divine? Think about the concept of lengthy deceased family members viewing through life over you and directing you? I'm yes you have, We mean haven't all of us?

Well mine is, various.

For the full time that is longest I thought I became the only person who could notice it, no body else I experienced mentioned it to, had any clue of the things I was speaking of. Buddies and moms and dads simply assumed it had been a childish dream or even the hopeless aspire to see and experience the realm that is spiritual. Other people thought me personally crazy.

I'm maybe not crazy. I understand that sounds like something a person that is crazy say but some other person saw it. That thing, my guide it that is not an angel if you were to phone. It's a monster. It wasn't until the age ended up being reached by me of twenty-two that another person finally noticed it. For the past twenty-one many years I happened to be the only person who spotted the thing that is damn around watching me personally. Tormenting me.

It all started the I happened to be born, We wasn't supposed to live past childbirth, one thing wanted me personally dead, and it has been attempting ever since day. My birth ended up being unpleasant to say the least, especially for my mommy. Upon finally birth that is offering seen the health practitioners cut the umbilical cord from about my neck and push myself away from her waiting hands.

I became basically dead, strangled to the point I no longer sucked within the environment this is certainly bleached. After around half a complete-time they wheeled me back to the area with what i could just believe to be an incubator of types. If you don't for the technology of modern-day i'd likely have-been lifeless time.

This is certainly except for one thing, a sound like all folks we don't understand that day. Initial sound that is real heard only moments before my heart restarted.

I no more understand what it said, and truthfully I don't think I want to know what it stated once I was plumped for because of it. Nevertheless, I recall the appear to be wheezing breaths combined with a gurgling this is certainly sickly of and bloodstream. It plagues me every and has now when it comes to past twenty-two years night.

Skip ahead to my year this is certainly 2nd of life and once even more death arrived for me personally. Becoming the adventurous and child that is fascinated was I suckled a marble-like a bonbon: of course this is extremely dangerous and stupid of me personally.

According to my knowledge, the marble had been stuck. during my throat and my moms and dads which can be frantic every thing to release the cup orb gradually draining the life from their child before them; from my throat.

They attempted every little thing, even going as far as pushing their hands into my throat in an attempt that is vain make me puke the marble out, only to view it slip deeper down. Until unexpectedly we spat it without concern. To this day they are nonetheless bewildered by the miracle we performed but it was know it wasn't because that is when I initially saw it n't me.

Perhaps not completely, I think which was its decision as to not frighten the living daylight from me personally. We saw its fingers to my shoulders: long bony hands curled down gently tapping prodigious claws to my tender flesh, grey skin stretched tightly over the scrawny bones tightening and groaning with every stretch and faucet upon my epidermis. We don't know why however it calmed myself instead of frightening me personally, perhaps because of my lack of glimpsing the animal.

Time passed relatively properly after that I'd no telephone calls that are close near-death experiences and every little thing seemed typical. Really there is one disturbance that is strange my third birthday however it's totally coincidental.

I guess i ought to describe this instead of bypassing it: back at my birthday that is third thirty-first of October, only one youngster knocked on our home to deceive or treat. One young child ended up being uncommon in those days but not unusual, however the part this is certainly strangest ended up being exactly what he said to my moms and dads once they asked where in fact the various other children were.

The boy around five or six merely pointed to the roofing simply close to the chimney that has been today highlighted by the moon that is full said. "The unusual guy on the top is frightening all of them away." Needless to say no mother or father desires to hear this from any person so logically my dad checked the roofing. He found absolutely nothing of course, which just made things worse, causing all of them to blatantly ignore the door's rings later on that night.

The next handful of years passed away relatively safely with no close this is certainly real or near-death experiences nor any dubious circumstances.

That was until one autumn morning, me personally and my sis: 36 months above the age of me and created on Friday the thirteenth; were planning college this is certainly primary the coach with your mum. I happened to be sucking in a sweet: those purple and white swirly ones which can be hard-boiled and flavor of ointment and strawberry. Anyway I became sucking on one of those and instantly demise saw their possibility once again through choking when I ended up being saying.

I lurched forward as the delicious rushed down my throat and stuck itself within its limits, trying to spit it out as my eyes began to liquidize. My sibling panicked, slapping my right back furiously as my mum rose, pulling myself up to smack my back.

Smacking it more difficult with each strike she grimaced, wanting to force it out by pulling her fists into my stomach and slamming me into her; at this true point my head had begun to enlarge somewhat with force and my epidermis began to turn blue. My lips became colder as tingles, almost like icy rain, danced across my fingers and palms, my vision clouded, and the noises around me faded away except for a few things. The terrified screams of my sister while the pressing this is certainly high-pitched of tongue.

Folks regarding the coach stared in silence whilst the driver continued their course, people saw as my mum struggled to save myself, her son dying before her as she saw. Rips streamed from her face pouring down her cheeks to drench my throat as she tried to remain composed. Rotating me dramatically she apologized before ramming her hands down my neck and holding them there.

I gagged as I heaved and lurched, felt the contents of my stomach churn and gurgle as my vision darkened, the glimpse this is certainly minor of skinned arms back at my mother's flooded my vision because they forced her fingers further. Unexpectedly and violently we vomited spraying my stomach's items across the flooring and myself to the chorus that is ridiculous of through the various other individuals, have been quickly silenced by my mother's hatred filled glare.

Her arms covered in spite of the sick coating my uniform as I gasped gulping in atmosphere greedily watching the hands slide from my mother's shoulders, to slide back down the bus; each lengthy digit slipping throughout the chairs plastic gum covered handlebars before scraping down the textile of the final group of chairs around me adopting me.

After that demise appeared to have abandoned trying to rob me personally of air rather choosing to you will need to hit me personally with cars or ravage me with puppies and push myself off steep hills and into lakes. Time passed like a stray puppy emitting a necrotic stench enjoy it would for almost any son or daughter yet that near-death experience from the coach accompanied myself.

We only believe returning to it into the individual that is third I'm watching myself die. However strangely sufficient the creature is vacant from the memory however it is understood by myself ended up being there saving myself yet again, but the reason why? Does it prey on my power? My heart? I honestly don't know however it's maintaining myself alive, and I don't know the reason why.

Many years passed away by pals came and moved and I caught glimpses associated with creature, constantly glimpses never the point that is full. It desired us to however understand it had been there, but not I'd like to see it. On days, I would personally catch it behind woods only peeking round viewing myself, its skin this is certainly grey seemingly within the sunshine than during the night. Large milky eyes that are white at me for as long emaciated arms hung down touching the ground. Every one twitched slightly while the moments passed.

In other cases I would hear it muttering or whispering as if speaking with another person only to develop silent when I glanced over at the path associated with the sounds. Every so often, it could be thought by myself. That way feeling you can't quite explain whenever you know some body is seeing you but they're when you look at the area that is same you merely not noticeable.

Fundamentally nights became nightmares, shadows danced on the wall space of my area, flickering like jittery creatures constantly convulsing and twitching as they dry heaved and scuttled about on spindly legs covered in wiry hairs. The light associated with street would abruptly dim, making me go through the window simply to find a shadow quickly disappear from the glow that is ominous of moon that would crawl in through the blinds.

Then came the determining; the sensation from it watching me personally, perhaps not from throughout the offered space but directly behind me. I might awake from rest absolutely terrified with broad eyes and shaking lips like I became nevertheless resting, only to sit staring at the wall in addition to shadows upon it when I pushed myself to act. I would personally set truth be told there seeing whilst the forms relocated, increasing greater, depicting a relative mind slightly elongated and practically crescent-shaped in appearance like a moon tilted sideways.

a mass this is certainly black move rising higher across the wall reaching over myself before splitting by 50 percent, the dangling appendages and tendril-like veins snapping collectively to entangle and produce elongated hands that stretched and crept closer.

I really could feel its breath from the back of my throat, perhaps not hot like a full time income creature but cool, ice-cold, no cold that is freezing. Cold to your real point, chills would run along my back and my hairs would stand up using the goosebumps covering my epidermis like sores. Odd arcane whispers seeped from its jaws associated with the stench of fermented liquid and damp leaves tainted with a foul smell that is pungent of skin.

Squishing my eyes closed tightly ended up being the reprieve that is just had from that torment since it plucked and fed upon my fear, likely suckling down the sweet nectar in pleasure. Its tongue this is certainly leaking swirling lapping at the droplets hanging from the claws.

These instances however had been quickly changed with brilliant ambitions of torture performed by nightmarish ghouls and beings which can be demonic. Each one of an nature that is otherworldly vaguely anthropomorphic statures with crowned skulls riddled with rivets and spines of twisted material.

Hopes and dreams of being burned alive and eaten by bark covered figures with glowing eyes which can be crimson little black colored irises that orbited smouldering orange pupils haunted me. Their particular jaws chomping down to my muscle that is revealed and pulling it tight to stretch it out and ring it of its juices since it tore away, snapping with unnatural elasticity.

Tiny beings like spiders covered in bony bristles crawled across my own body. This is certainly nude it with tiny pincers while they relocated burrowing into every orifice. Their little types squirming under my eyelids and chewing through my eardrums to pull webs across my mind, blanketing it in a foggy haze similar to a trance that is hypnotic.

The worst had been the haunting spectral visions associated with the tree that plagued me personally both night and day; its kind rising up into a purple that is deep red sky housing eclipsed suns of green fire. Bat-like animals hung from the tree's limbs, squeaking with delight silver-eyes and frilled pointed ears, membranes of human faces hugged their bodies with silvery eyes that boiled the blood pumping throughout my real type while they stared at me.

Giant eight legged beings sat in webs strewn from individual intestines that continuously dripped blood on the bundled up kiddies below caught like flies. The beings laughed, muttering in alien tongues or old and languages that are arcane pictures of cyclopean places to flash in my front lobe. Their arms waved around, each one coated in severed fingers that are man twitched and writhed in agony. Eyes of bare black voids stared down on me from atop the gluey traps and bodies which can be bulbous.

The tree breathed deeply, drawing at a negative balance mist of bloodstream from the air, its origins pulsing and flickering with ghastly green and light that is pink with a hue of magenta and red. Fell voices called aside lullabies that are singing my ears, urging myself closer as a hand rested on my neck, hefty and grey directing me toward the tree.

My eyes would break open with a shout as sweat poured out of every pore that is feasible, soaking my clothes and drenching my bedsheets as I panted feverishly, quivering in abstract scary. Rest served me no sanctuary through the animal. Nor from the masters and minions.

I went to a shrink when, he explained it had been a stage and merely signs and symptoms of an imagination this is certainly overactive. We have that, but this is simply not that, this will be hell itself taunting me. Some sort of divine punishment for living, for escaping demise and enduring. Of making a mockery of these who would call themselves gods.

Recently though I came across camping eased my mind a lot more than my personal space. Something about becoming confronted with nature somehow calmed my aspirations and visions along with my putting up with mind. Well, it performed for the right time however it led to something worse, much worse.

2-3 weeks in a forest, this forest nonetheless is reported to be certainly one of the UK's most troubled woodlands with a few murder instances unsolved and lots of lacking reports ago I invited a pal to camp beside me. Being the paranormal and cryptic fans we are, we thought it was the most perfect location for a ghost hunt and examination that is paranormal.

We brought what we required: tents, resting bags, torches etc. You know the camping that is normal. I also got my arms on an emergency success system that held rations, a striker and flint, liquid purification pills, you know that type of things. Made myself feel it absolutely was really worth buying like I happened to be preparing for an apocalypse having all of this stuff but nonetheless.

After visiting the forest, we invested the day perambulating, laughing and generally becoming stupid, picking right up twigs pretending to have sword battles or trying art this is certainly martial. Which we failed poorly and I indicate poorly. We tested the pills to get the liquid surprisingly refreshing in spite of the slight taste that is metallic in the water. I guess these tablets just do this much and haven't already been upgraded to make it taste better.

We took images on a camera this is certainly a throwaway to get a photo of Bigfoot or a ghost. During the time, we hadn't noticed, but we caught things i can't nearly describe, Atlanta divorce attorneys photo there were figures which were not at all here when we took the pictures on their own.

The numbers showed up practically transparent which genuinely scared the shit out of me additionally really got me personally hyped. I am talking about we really caught evidence of spirits! The night came faster we create camp, making a fire in a small set of trees shaped in a circle, we laughed and joked despite the creep aspect washing in like a thick fog than we anticipated therefore.

The emphasis of our trip really originated in finding a bag of candies into the crisis success kit, childish I'm sure, but they had been a variety of boiled and sweets which can be smooth.

Then things got weird, truly strange, eerily weird. Firstly it was simply the sensation like we had been being seen, then something terrifying happened. A scream had been heard by us. not merely an easy old. "Ow my toe!" Kind of shout, this is somebody screaming murder this is certainly bloody of shout.

To help make matters more serious, it absolutely was a woman's that is blood-curdling coming from someplace deep in the woods. My friend jumped up shining a torch into the trees while he whispered. "Did you hear that is just fucking?"

Sitting up slowly and hiding the fear flooding that i obviously heard it and therefore it had been probably just a fox through myself i answered telling him. It's scary, no joke they appear to be babies sobbing or females screaming in the event that you've never heard a fox at night.

He refused to think my opinion than him, but I'll confess I happened to be in the same way frightened as him and happy he had been alert not so glad he had been shining the torch into the woods despite me having even more understanding on pets. Today we don't here get wolves or bears so when he stated. "I believe we see eyes over here." I shit myself.

Leaping up we swallowed driving a car lodged in my neck after his finger that is pointed and torches light, reduced and behold there was clearly anything showing the light like eyes. Today this terrified us to my core, absolutely nothing must certainly be doing that out here, and those weren't eyes which are deer these were also close together for that. This was demonstrably predatory, my mind raced thinking to the stories of huge cats in the country that is UK The Rake: that thing scared the crap away from me personally.

We watched the eyes for at least an hour we decided that perhaps we must keep and not exposure keeping the night time before they just vanished into the trees without an audio, revealing a glance. Making up our thoughts and collecting our things we dismissed the distant screams of feasible foxes or ladies whilst the forests grew quiet, too quiet.

It is whenever they go quiet it's a bad indication once you learn such a thing about forests. It means some thing is around that's dangerous. Noticing this I straightened staring down to the trees as my pal stuffed everything into the bags with a messy hurried activity; not that we blamed him. Then my heart dropped, my buddy no more filled the bags at him alternatively he was staring off into the woods, his eyes wider than We have ever seen to the point I thought they'd burst down as I glanced.

Their human body trembled violently and not to shame him, but he had pissed himself, he said I would personally have done the exact same if we had seen what. Leaning ahead he had been asked by me the thing that was wrong before shining my light to the woods he was transfixed on; tears streamed down their face as he whispered. "We need to go."

"Okay?" I said helping him grab the stuff while he cried, catching my hand.

"We need to get now, keep this crap here we have to go!" Concerned and terrified we obliged, grabbing just what was needed even as we glanced around even as we relocated, almost holding arms.

Moving toward the path regarding the automobile, we heard footsteps and twigs snapping, making us go faster and much more anxiously even as we rapidly moved into a sprint virtually scuba diving in to the vehicle and whacking the headlights to beam that is full the vehicle park.

"What's wrong? Just what do you see?" I asked fearing for my entire life that is friend's and very own as he proceeded to cry somewhat.

Today my buddy never cries out of worry so to essentially see this made me nervous. Waiting around for his reply I scanned the woods for activity recently catching a glimpse of something going behind a tree, the form of a leg that is human, its claws dragging over the surface behind it. My eyes widened as my pal muttered to himself, pushing his face into his fingers given that animal paused switching it had been at that point I noticed its full look toward me with a grin.

The animal stood around eight-foot tall at the least. Its skin was grey this is certainly pale, nearly clear, exposing the organs below as well as the pulsing hearts of black muscle tissue beating within. Glowing white-eyes stared straight back at me as a grin this is certainly thin the needle like teeth jutting straight down from its jaws. Its face ended up being thin, gaunt and yet this is certainly tight individual. Lengthy arms that are scrawny by its part coming in contact with the ground as long digitigrade legs covered in tight flesh supported its emaciated human anatomy. Big black colored wings being feathered with clawed fingers hung down from its back partially collapsed to full cover up the row of spiny protrusions sticking aside along its backbone.

My eyes declined to blink because it stared at me personally smiling while they burned screaming at me personally. Its hand that is no-cost rising its lips to wipe away the dark patches of moisture glistening around its slim lips. My human body trembled since the creature smiled wickedly pushing skin to split along its face allowing its jaws to show the majesty this is certainly filled with maw stretching halfway up its head.

We stammered attempting to talk due to the fact creature switched waving over its shoulder to head into the forests aided by the physical human body of someone. It can only be a week later it had was a known rapist and murderer that has escaped authorities in your community that We discovered that the guy.

Once you understand this now tends to make me sick to my tummy and has now ended me from going anywhere near more forests. We drove residence hushed and shaking until my pal were able to tell me what he saw, I never told him the thing I saw. I did son't want to frighten him any more than he currently was.

"I, I saw one thing. A creature." We glanced at him talking.

"What, like a fox or a wolf?" He declined to make as his eyes grew redder with their words which are tempered.

"No perhaps not a fucking fox!" He swallowed loudly. "It ended up being a person at first." That made my jaw drop as I thought back into the actual body the animal had.

"He had been viewing us, only smiling like a creep. Then…" his words trailed faraway from him once again as he sucked back once again the tears and snot harmful to drip.

"Then something came out of this trees behind him. Only selected him up because of the neck." We sat filled and silent with fear of just what would come next. "It didn't even watch out of the straight back of their mind! at me, only lifted a hand, and dug a finger right through their attention pressing it" My friend paused quickly, drawing in a breath that is shaky stuttering.

"I, I guessed he passed away instantly he attempted to fight while he didn't scream but then. That just made the plain thing smile." He considered myself. "It fucking smiled!" My heart skipped a beat with that terrible grin like a demonic shark as I imagined it working up alongside the vehicle to touch regarding the screen to laugh at me personally.

"That's when it gripped his supply ripping it off like, like, IT TORE IT OFF!" his sudden yell broke my train of idea with silver light when I glanced at the moon shining down on us. "It then clamped its jaws around their face-smashing it, I heard the bone crack!" he whispered, peering over we rubbed a shaky hand across my eyebrow at me personally since.

"Just keep operating and get us away from here and to the city, be safer it'll. Then we can go to the police,as he snorted, grasping the wheel with a white-knuckle grip" I said, wanting to remain as peaceful as you are able to.

"They won't believe us, they'll say we're on drugs or that we killed him. We'll be sent to a nut home and locked up." Just as much it he was right nobody would think us as I hated to admit.

We remained silent for the remainder journey residence, each of us anxiously staring from the house windows snapping our heads around at the sound this is certainly the slightest or light of a driving car. We had been petrified plus it revealed evidently when we got stopped for speeding.

A few cops asked us the questions which are normal. "Have you taken medicines, have you drank liquor this? evening" We lied telling all of them we'd a grouped family emergency however they didn't fully get it. I could tell if they went off to talk to each other about our panicked condition and terror this is certainly clear-eyes.

Ultimately they let us carry on a caution stating they might shadow us to another city then we were to attend our "emergency" then straight residence. Hmph home, that way does something that knows in which we lived. I just hoped it didn't understand where he lived.

Luckily my concern was answered when my pal labeled as me telling me everything is fine and he is getting over them as best he can for now anyway night. I've been to test he refused to answer the door and has now caught to keeping every blind or curtain shut on him but.

I haven't informed him that I saw the basic thing on their roof once. Primarily because i do believe it absolutely was simply after me because I don't know how to make sure he understands additionally. I experienced seen it stalking me from the rooftops, jumping from every one with a grace that is strange peeking within the chimneys.

We haven't discussed this to anyone either, but I'm having a dream this is certainly new i do believe it's my demise, or at the very least my limbo? Hell? We don't know. We don't even have to sleep to begin to see the fantasy either, I simply shut my eyes and there I are.

Imagine a field or vast available expanse of land, now shroud that land in a thick fog this is certainly grey that on an autumn morning. Now imagine trees being black and devoid of leaves showing up when you look at the fog but remove the trunks and look at the branches stretching on like veins of black colored bloodstream across the sky. That's where we am, and there's no sunlight, no light with no sounds except one, the breath this is certainly wheezing first heard when I came to be.

The animal is known by me is behind me personally into the dream waiting. Expecting us to run, but I believe it is useless, this thing features followed me all my entire life now like a classic buddy if I pass away I am going to welcome it. Ideally.

It's previous midnight today when I write this, I'm terrified. The hopes and dreams have actually ended just now replaced with something notably worse, much worse. I'm trying to not look it knows I am aware it's indeed there seeing me compose at it but. It's in my room, sitting in the desk by my window.

I will see its wings obviously now from my peripheral vision. What exactly I thought were feathers are in fact person arms with hundreds of fingers covered in finely feathers which are put. Its eyes are dim sucking into the light through the landing therefore the street outside, no not the road. The road is gone, replaced with a sky this is certainly crimson. I am able to see the moon eclipsed in the sky, spilling a hue that is red the atmosphere. I'm able to begin to see the tree and hear the animals which are bat-like. I'm terrified.

Kindly for me personally or it if you check this out don't appearance. After you have already been chosen, indeed there is no escaping. You are happy if you have never experienced a near-death knowledge. I do believe it nourishes regarding the life i should have had n't. The greater I try to withstand looking the harder it gets.

It is shifting now, rolling its arms and massaging its neck want it's aching or bored from only watching me. Its teeth tend to be chattering, oh god it's eating an infant!

I will. "Oh, no, no, no it is nonetheless alive!" We can't help myself. I need to look. "No! I'm perhaps not ready to die; we don't would you like to go!"

It's five in the now morning. It stopped eating around three. I looked over me personally and spoke at it and it just smiled. Its voice had been putrid, sluggish and whispery however gruff like gravel grinding together and rock bone tissue this is certainly breaking. Gargles of blood and puss accompanied the wheezing as it savoured them telling me personally as it talked, dragging out each word.

"You tend to be safe, my kid. Father is here now."

The Irish countryside is being haunted by an ancient horror.

Have you ever heard the thought of nature guides or protectors which can be divine? Think about the concept of lengthy deceased family members viewing through life over you and directing you? I'm yes you have, We mean haven't all of us?

Well mine is, various.

For the full time that is longest I thought I became the only person who could notice it, no body else I experienced mentioned it to, had any clue of the things I was speaking of. Buddies and moms and dads simply assumed it had been a childish dream or even the hopeless aspire to see and experience the realm that is spiritual. Other people thought me personally crazy.

I'm maybe not crazy. I understand that sounds like something a person that is crazy say but some other person saw it. That thing, my guide it that is not an angel if you were to phone. It's a monster. It wasn't until the age ended up being reached by me of twenty-two that another person finally noticed it. For the past twenty-one many years I happened to be the only person who spotted the thing that is damn around watching me personally. Tormenting me.

It all started the I happened to be born, We wasn't supposed to live past childbirth, one thing wanted me personally dead, and it has been attempting ever since day. My birth ended up being unpleasant to say the least, especially for my mommy. Upon finally birth that is offering seen the health practitioners cut the umbilical cord from about my neck and push myself away from her waiting hands.

I became basically dead, strangled to the point I no longer sucked within the environment this is certainly bleached. After around half a complete-time they wheeled me back to the area with what i could just believe to be an incubator of types. If you don't for the technology of modern-day i'd likely have-been lifeless time.

This is certainly except for one thing, a sound like all folks we don't understand that day. Initial sound that is real heard only moments before my heart restarted.

I no more understand what it said, and truthfully I don't think I want to know what it stated once I was plumped for because of it. Nevertheless, I recall the appear to be wheezing breaths combined with a gurgling this is certainly sickly of and bloodstream. It plagues me every and has now when it comes to past twenty-two years night.

Skip ahead to my year this is certainly 2nd of life and once even more death arrived for me personally. Becoming the adventurous and child that is fascinated was I suckled a marble-like a bonbon: of course this is extremely dangerous and stupid of me personally.

According to my knowledge, the marble had been stuck. during my throat and my moms and dads which can be frantic every thing to release the cup orb gradually draining the life from their child before them; from my throat.

They attempted every little thing, even going as far as pushing their hands into my throat in an attempt that is vain make me puke the marble out, only to view it slip deeper down. Until unexpectedly we spat it without concern. To this day they are nonetheless bewildered by the miracle we performed but it was know it wasn't because that is when I initially saw it n't me.

Perhaps not completely, I think which was its decision as to not frighten the living daylight from me personally. We saw its fingers to my shoulders: long bony hands curled down gently tapping prodigious claws to my tender flesh, grey skin stretched tightly over the scrawny bones tightening and groaning with every stretch and faucet upon my epidermis. We don't know why however it calmed myself instead of frightening me personally, perhaps because of my lack of glimpsing the animal.

Time passed relatively properly after that I'd no telephone calls that are close near-death experiences and every little thing seemed typical. Really there is one disturbance that is strange my third birthday however it's totally coincidental.

I guess i ought to describe this instead of bypassing it: back at my birthday that is third thirty-first of October, only one youngster knocked on our home to deceive or treat. One young child ended up being uncommon in those days but not unusual, however the part this is certainly strangest ended up being exactly what he said to my moms and dads once they asked where in fact the various other children were.

The boy around five or six merely pointed to the roofing simply close to the chimney that has been today highlighted by the moon that is full said. "The unusual guy on the top is frightening all of them away." Needless to say no mother or father desires to hear this from any person so logically my dad checked the roofing. He found absolutely nothing of course, which just made things worse, causing all of them to blatantly ignore the door's rings later on that night.

The next handful of years passed away relatively safely with no close this is certainly real or near-death experiences nor any dubious circumstances.

That was until one autumn morning, me personally and my sis: 36 months above the age of me and created on Friday the thirteenth; were planning college this is certainly primary the coach with your mum. I happened to be sucking in a sweet: those purple and white swirly ones which can be hard-boiled and flavor of ointment and strawberry. Anyway I became sucking on one of those and instantly demise saw their possibility once again through choking when I ended up being saying.

I lurched forward as the delicious rushed down my throat and stuck itself within its limits, trying to spit it out as my eyes began to liquidize. My sibling panicked, slapping my right back furiously as my mum rose, pulling myself up to smack my back.

Smacking it more difficult with each strike she grimaced, wanting to force it out by pulling her fists into my stomach and slamming me into her; at this true point my head had begun to enlarge somewhat with force and my epidermis began to turn blue. My lips became colder as tingles, almost like icy rain, danced across my fingers and palms, my vision clouded, and the noises around me faded away except for a few things. The terrified screams of my sister while the pressing this is certainly high-pitched of tongue.

Folks regarding the coach stared in silence whilst the driver continued their course, people saw as my mum struggled to save myself, her son dying before her as she saw. Rips streamed from her face pouring down her cheeks to drench my throat as she tried to remain composed. Rotating me dramatically she apologized before ramming her hands down my neck and holding them there.

I gagged as I heaved and lurched, felt the contents of my stomach churn and gurgle as my vision darkened, the glimpse this is certainly minor of skinned arms back at my mother's flooded my vision because they forced her fingers further. Unexpectedly and violently we vomited spraying my stomach's items across the flooring and myself to the chorus that is ridiculous of through the various other individuals, have been quickly silenced by my mother's hatred filled glare.

Her arms covered in spite of the sick coating my uniform as I gasped gulping in atmosphere greedily watching the hands slide from my mother's shoulders, to slide back down the bus; each lengthy digit slipping throughout the chairs plastic gum covered handlebars before scraping down the textile of the final group of chairs around me adopting me.

After that demise appeared to have abandoned trying to rob me personally of air rather choosing to you will need to hit me personally with cars or ravage me with puppies and push myself off steep hills and into lakes. Time passed like a stray puppy emitting a necrotic stench enjoy it would for almost any son or daughter yet that near-death experience from the coach accompanied myself.

We only believe returning to it into the individual that is third I'm watching myself die. However strangely sufficient the creature is vacant from the memory however it is understood by myself ended up being there saving myself yet again, but the reason why? Does it prey on my power? My heart? I honestly don't know however it's maintaining myself alive, and I don't know the reason why.

Many years passed away by pals came and moved and I caught glimpses associated with creature, constantly glimpses never the point that is full. It desired us to however understand it had been there, but not I'd like to see it. On days, I would personally catch it behind woods only peeking round viewing myself, its skin this is certainly grey seemingly within the sunshine than during the night. Large milky eyes that are white at me for as long emaciated arms hung down touching the ground. Every one twitched slightly while the moments passed.

In other cases I would hear it muttering or whispering as if speaking with another person only to develop silent when I glanced over at the path associated with the sounds. Every so often, it could be thought by myself. That way feeling you can't quite explain whenever you know some body is seeing you but they're when you look at the area that is same you merely not noticeable.

Fundamentally nights became nightmares, shadows danced on the wall space of my area, flickering like jittery creatures constantly convulsing and twitching as they dry heaved and scuttled about on spindly legs covered in wiry hairs. The light associated with street would abruptly dim, making me go through the window simply to find a shadow quickly disappear from the glow that is ominous of moon that would crawl in through the blinds.

Then came the determining; the sensation from it watching me personally, perhaps not from throughout the offered space but directly behind me. I might awake from rest absolutely terrified with broad eyes and shaking lips like I became nevertheless resting, only to sit staring at the wall in addition to shadows upon it when I pushed myself to act. I would personally set truth be told there seeing whilst the forms relocated, increasing greater, depicting a relative mind slightly elongated and practically crescent-shaped in appearance like a moon tilted sideways.

a mass this is certainly black move rising higher across the wall reaching over myself before splitting by 50 percent, the dangling appendages and tendril-like veins snapping collectively to entangle and produce elongated hands that stretched and crept closer.

I really could feel its breath from the back of my throat, perhaps not hot like a full time income creature but cool, ice-cold, no cold that is freezing. Cold to your real point, chills would run along my back and my hairs would stand up using the goosebumps covering my epidermis like sores. Odd arcane whispers seeped from its jaws associated with the stench of fermented liquid and damp leaves tainted with a foul smell that is pungent of skin.

Squishing my eyes closed tightly ended up being the reprieve that is just had from that torment since it plucked and fed upon my fear, likely suckling down the sweet nectar in pleasure. Its tongue this is certainly leaking swirling lapping at the droplets hanging from the claws.

These instances however had been quickly changed with brilliant ambitions of torture performed by nightmarish ghouls and beings which can be demonic. Each one of an nature that is otherworldly vaguely anthropomorphic statures with crowned skulls riddled with rivets and spines of twisted material.

Hopes and dreams of being burned alive and eaten by bark covered figures with glowing eyes which can be crimson little black colored irises that orbited smouldering orange pupils haunted me. Their particular jaws chomping down to my muscle that is revealed and pulling it tight to stretch it out and ring it of its juices since it tore away, snapping with unnatural elasticity.

Tiny beings like spiders covered in bony bristles crawled across my own body. This is certainly nude it with tiny pincers while they relocated burrowing into every orifice. Their little types squirming under my eyelids and chewing through my eardrums to pull webs across my mind, blanketing it in a foggy haze similar to a trance that is hypnotic.

The worst had been the haunting spectral visions associated with the tree that plagued me personally both night and day; its kind rising up into a purple that is deep red sky housing eclipsed suns of green fire. Bat-like animals hung from the tree's limbs, squeaking with delight silver-eyes and frilled pointed ears, membranes of human faces hugged their bodies with silvery eyes that boiled the blood pumping throughout my real type while they stared at me.

Giant eight legged beings sat in webs strewn from individual intestines that continuously dripped blood on the bundled up kiddies below caught like flies. The beings laughed, muttering in alien tongues or old and languages that are arcane pictures of cyclopean places to flash in my front lobe. Their arms waved around, each one coated in severed fingers that are man twitched and writhed in agony. Eyes of bare black voids stared down on me from atop the gluey traps and bodies which can be bulbous.

The tree breathed deeply, drawing at a negative balance mist of bloodstream from the air, its origins pulsing and flickering with ghastly green and light that is pink with a hue of magenta and red. Fell voices called aside lullabies that are singing my ears, urging myself closer as a hand rested on my neck, hefty and grey directing me toward the tree.

My eyes would break open with a shout as sweat poured out of every pore that is feasible, soaking my clothes and drenching my bedsheets as I panted feverishly, quivering in abstract scary. Rest served me no sanctuary through the animal. Nor from the masters and minions.

I went to a shrink when, he explained it had been a stage and merely signs and symptoms of an imagination this is certainly overactive. We have that, but this is simply not that, this will be hell itself taunting me. Some sort of divine punishment for living, for escaping demise and enduring. Of making a mockery of these who would call themselves gods.

Recently though I came across camping eased my mind a lot more than my personal space. Something about becoming confronted with nature somehow calmed my aspirations and visions along with my putting up with mind. Well, it performed for the right time however it led to something worse, much worse.

2-3 weeks in a forest, this forest nonetheless is reported to be certainly one of the UK's most troubled woodlands with a few murder instances unsolved and lots of lacking reports ago I invited a pal to camp beside me. Being the paranormal and cryptic fans we are, we thought it was the most perfect location for a ghost hunt and examination that is paranormal.

We brought what we required: tents, resting bags, torches etc. You know the camping that is normal. I also got my arms on an emergency success system that held rations, a striker and flint, liquid purification pills, you know that type of things. Made myself feel it absolutely was really worth buying like I happened to be preparing for an apocalypse having all of this stuff but nonetheless.

After visiting the forest, we invested the day perambulating, laughing and generally becoming stupid, picking right up twigs pretending to have sword battles or trying art this is certainly martial. Which we failed poorly and I indicate poorly. We tested the pills to get the liquid surprisingly refreshing in spite of the slight taste that is metallic in the water. I guess these tablets just do this much and haven't already been upgraded to make it taste better.

We took images on a camera this is certainly a throwaway to get a photo of Bigfoot or a ghost. During the time, we hadn't noticed, but we caught things i can't nearly describe, Atlanta divorce attorneys photo there were figures which were not at all here when we took the pictures on their own.

The numbers showed up practically transparent which genuinely scared the shit out of me additionally really got me personally hyped. I am talking about we really caught evidence of spirits! The night came faster we create camp, making a fire in a small set of trees shaped in a circle, we laughed and joked despite the creep aspect washing in like a thick fog than we anticipated therefore.

The emphasis of our trip really originated in finding a bag of candies into the crisis success kit, childish I'm sure, but they had been a variety of boiled and sweets which can be smooth.

Then things got weird, truly strange, eerily weird. Firstly it was simply the sensation like we had been being seen, then something terrifying happened. A scream had been heard by us. not merely an easy old. "Ow my toe!" Kind of shout, this is somebody screaming murder this is certainly bloody of shout.

To help make matters more serious, it absolutely was a woman's that is blood-curdling coming from someplace deep in the woods. My friend jumped up shining a torch into the trees while he whispered. "Did you hear that is just fucking?"

Sitting up slowly and hiding the fear flooding that i obviously heard it and therefore it had been probably just a fox through myself i answered telling him. It's scary, no joke they appear to be babies sobbing or females screaming in the event that you've never heard a fox at night.

He refused to think my opinion than him, but I'll confess I happened to be in the same way frightened as him and happy he had been alert not so glad he had been shining the torch into the woods despite me having even more understanding on pets. Today we don't here get wolves or bears so when he stated. "I believe we see eyes over here." I shit myself.

Leaping up we swallowed driving a car lodged in my neck after his finger that is pointed and torches light, reduced and behold there was clearly anything showing the light like eyes. Today this terrified us to my core, absolutely nothing must certainly be doing that out here, and those weren't eyes which are deer these were also close together for that. This was demonstrably predatory, my mind raced thinking to the stories of huge cats in the country that is UK The Rake: that thing scared the crap away from me personally.

We watched the eyes for at least an hour we decided that perhaps we must keep and not exposure keeping the night time before they just vanished into the trees without an audio, revealing a glance. Making up our thoughts and collecting our things we dismissed the distant screams of feasible foxes or ladies whilst the forests grew quiet, too quiet.

It is whenever they go quiet it's a bad indication once you learn such a thing about forests. It means some thing is around that's dangerous. Noticing this I straightened staring down to the trees as my pal stuffed everything into the bags with a messy hurried activity; not that we blamed him. Then my heart dropped, my buddy no more filled the bags at him alternatively he was staring off into the woods, his eyes wider than We have ever seen to the point I thought they'd burst down as I glanced.

Their human body trembled violently and not to shame him, but he had pissed himself, he said I would personally have done the exact same if we had seen what. Leaning ahead he had been asked by me the thing that was wrong before shining my light to the woods he was transfixed on; tears streamed down their face as he whispered. "We need to go."

"Okay?" I said helping him grab the stuff while he cried, catching my hand.

"We need to get now, keep this crap here we have to go!" Concerned and terrified we obliged, grabbing just what was needed even as we glanced around even as we relocated, almost holding arms.

Moving toward the path regarding the automobile, we heard footsteps and twigs snapping, making us go faster and much more anxiously even as we rapidly moved into a sprint virtually scuba diving in to the vehicle and whacking the headlights to beam that is full the vehicle park.

"What's wrong? Just what do you see?" I asked fearing for my entire life that is friend's and very own as he proceeded to cry somewhat.

Today my buddy never cries out of worry so to essentially see this made me nervous. Waiting around for his reply I scanned the woods for activity recently catching a glimpse of something going behind a tree, the form of a leg that is human, its claws dragging over the surface behind it. My eyes widened as my pal muttered to himself, pushing his face into his fingers given that animal paused switching it had been at that point I noticed its full look toward me with a grin.

The animal stood around eight-foot tall at the least. Its skin was grey this is certainly pale, nearly clear, exposing the organs below as well as the pulsing hearts of black muscle tissue beating within. Glowing white-eyes stared straight back at me as a grin this is certainly thin the needle like teeth jutting straight down from its jaws. Its face ended up being thin, gaunt and yet this is certainly tight individual. Lengthy arms that are scrawny by its part coming in contact with the ground as long digitigrade legs covered in tight flesh supported its emaciated human anatomy. Big black colored wings being feathered with clawed fingers hung down from its back partially collapsed to full cover up the row of spiny protrusions sticking aside along its backbone.

My eyes declined to blink because it stared at me personally smiling while they burned screaming at me personally. Its hand that is no-cost rising its lips to wipe away the dark patches of moisture glistening around its slim lips. My human body trembled since the creature smiled wickedly pushing skin to split along its face allowing its jaws to show the majesty this is certainly filled with maw stretching halfway up its head.

We stammered attempting to talk due to the fact creature switched waving over its shoulder to head into the forests aided by the physical human body of someone. It can only be a week later it had was a known rapist and murderer that has escaped authorities in your community that We discovered that the guy.

Once you understand this now tends to make me sick to my tummy and has now ended me from going anywhere near more forests. We drove residence hushed and shaking until my pal were able to tell me what he saw, I never told him the thing I saw. I did son't want to frighten him any more than he currently was.

"I, I saw one thing. A creature." We glanced at him talking.

"What, like a fox or a wolf?" He declined to make as his eyes grew redder with their words which are tempered.

"No perhaps not a fucking fox!" He swallowed loudly. "It ended up being a person at first." That made my jaw drop as I thought back into the actual body the animal had.

"He had been viewing us, only smiling like a creep. Then…" his words trailed faraway from him once again as he sucked back once again the tears and snot harmful to drip.

"Then something came out of this trees behind him. Only selected him up because of the neck." We sat filled and silent with fear of just what would come next. "It didn't even watch out of the straight back of their mind! at me, only lifted a hand, and dug a finger right through their attention pressing it" My friend paused quickly, drawing in a breath that is shaky stuttering.

"I, I guessed he passed away instantly he attempted to fight while he didn't scream but then. That just made the plain thing smile." He considered myself. "It fucking smiled!" My heart skipped a beat with that terrible grin like a demonic shark as I imagined it working up alongside the vehicle to touch regarding the screen to laugh at me personally.

"That's when it gripped his supply ripping it off like, like, IT TORE IT OFF!" his sudden yell broke my train of idea with silver light when I glanced at the moon shining down on us. "It then clamped its jaws around their face-smashing it, I heard the bone crack!" he whispered, peering over we rubbed a shaky hand across my eyebrow at me personally since.

"Just keep operating and get us away from here and to the city, be safer it'll. Then we can go to the police,as he snorted, grasping the wheel with a white-knuckle grip" I said, wanting to remain as peaceful as you are able to.

"They won't believe us, they'll say we're on drugs or that we killed him. We'll be sent to a nut home and locked up." Just as much it he was right nobody would think us as I hated to admit.

We remained silent for the remainder journey residence, each of us anxiously staring from the house windows snapping our heads around at the sound this is certainly the slightest or light of a driving car. We had been petrified plus it revealed evidently when we got stopped for speeding.

A few cops asked us the questions which are normal. "Have you taken medicines, have you drank liquor this? evening" We lied telling all of them we'd a grouped family emergency however they didn't fully get it. I could tell if they went off to talk to each other about our panicked condition and terror this is certainly clear-eyes.

Ultimately they let us carry on a caution stating they might shadow us to another city then we were to attend our "emergency" then straight residence. Hmph home, that way does something that knows in which we lived. I just hoped it didn't understand where he lived.

Luckily my concern was answered when my pal labeled as me telling me everything is fine and he is getting over them as best he can for now anyway night. I've been to test he refused to answer the door and has now caught to keeping every blind or curtain shut on him but.

I haven't informed him that I saw the basic thing on their roof once. Primarily because i do believe it absolutely was simply after me because I don't know how to make sure he understands additionally. I experienced seen it stalking me from the rooftops, jumping from every one with a grace that is strange peeking within the chimneys.

We haven't discussed this to anyone either, but I'm having a dream this is certainly new i do believe it's my demise, or at the very least my limbo? Hell? We don't know. We don't even have to sleep to begin to see the fantasy either, I simply shut my eyes and there I are.

Imagine a field or vast available expanse of land, now shroud that land in a thick fog this is certainly grey that on an autumn morning. Now imagine trees being black and devoid of leaves showing up when you look at the fog but remove the trunks and look at the branches stretching on like veins of black colored bloodstream across the sky. That's where we am, and there's no sunlight, no light with no sounds except one, the breath this is certainly wheezing first heard when I came to be.

The animal is known by me is behind me personally into the dream waiting. Expecting us to run, but I believe it is useless, this thing features followed me all my entire life now like a classic buddy if I pass away I am going to welcome it. Ideally.

It's previous midnight today when I write this, I'm terrified. The hopes and dreams have actually ended just now replaced with something notably worse, much worse. I'm trying to not look it knows I am aware it's indeed there seeing me compose at it but. It's in my room, sitting in the desk by my window.

I will see its wings obviously now from my peripheral vision. What exactly I thought were feathers are in fact person arms with hundreds of fingers covered in finely feathers which are put. Its eyes are dim sucking into the light through the landing therefore the street outside, no not the road. The road is gone, replaced with a sky this is certainly crimson. I am able to see the moon eclipsed in the sky, spilling a hue that is red the atmosphere. I'm able to begin to see the tree and hear the animals which are bat-like. I'm terrified.

Kindly for me personally or it if you check this out don't appearance. After you have already been chosen, indeed there is no escaping. You are happy if you have never experienced a near-death knowledge. I do believe it nourishes regarding the life i should have had n't. The greater I try to withstand looking the harder it gets.

It is shifting now, rolling its arms and massaging its neck want it's aching or bored from only watching me. Its teeth tend to be chattering, oh god it's eating an infant!

I will. "Oh, no, no, no it is nonetheless alive!" We can't help myself. I need to look. "No! I'm perhaps not ready to die; we don't would you like to go!"

It's five in the now morning. It stopped eating around three. I looked over me personally and spoke at it and it just smiled. Its voice had been putrid, sluggish and whispery however gruff like gravel grinding together and rock bone tissue this is certainly breaking. Gargles of blood and puss accompanied the wheezing as it savoured them telling me personally as it talked, dragging out each word.

"You tend to be safe, my kid. Father is here now."